THE FIRE TREE
Book 4
THE DRAGON RINGS

by **Ken Kirk**

Dedicated to the memory of Pamela Lang,
Cydara Verrier,   Margaret Beatrice Kirk & Cecilia Reynolds.

2

PROLOGUE

The Story So Far...

This is Book 4 of *The Fire Tree* series. While Books 1 and 2 are standalone stories in their own right, Book 3 (*The Quickening*) directly precedes this tale. Here is what you need to know if you haven't read it...

The Ancient Legend

Eight hundred years ago, when the Vikings invaded Scotland, those who resisted were led by a remarkable Pictish warrior named Kiffan the Defiant. When she was captured and sentenced to death by the Viking King Urokmort, a great oak tree burst into flames. The tree burned for seven days and seven nights without consuming so much as a single leaf. Urokmort, terrified of angering the gods, spared Kiffan's life.

Kiffan became the first Queen of the West, founding a bloodline of warrior queens who would rule the Highlands for eight centuries. Since that miraculous day, the appearance of mystical flames has marked moments of great significance for her descendants, a sign that an ancient power watches over the Queens of the West and guides Scotland's destiny.

The Betrayal and Queen Cydara's Death

Seven years ago, after decades of bitter dispute, the powerful Clan Campbell returned to their seat at the Queen's Table. It was a historic moment of reconciliation, but it was a trap. Campbell traitors infiltrated the Queen's Honour Guard and murdered Queen Cydara in cold blood. They hunted for her daughter and heir, the twelve-year-old Princess Annis.

Annis was found hiding, but a brave man named Leslie threw himself between the assassins and the young princess, giving his life to save hers. His widow, Morag, despite her devastating loss, became a surrogate mother to Annis, never once showing resentment for the sacrifice her husband made.

At just twelve years old, Annis became the Queen of the West, inheriting a throne still warm from her mother's blood and a kingdom on the brink of chaos.

The Young Queen

The Dragon Rings

Now nineteen years old, Annis has spent seven years learning to be both queen and warrior. She is brave, compassionate, and fiercely determined to prove herself worthy of her crown. There are no account of how she might perform in true battle, leaving many clans watching her with sceptical eyes, wondering if she possesses the strength her mother had.

The Campbells, who murdered her mother, have not been brought to justice and remain a constant threat. King James of Scotland maintains an uneasy relationship with the Queen of the West, neither fully supporting nor openly opposing her ancient claim to rule the Highlands.

The Walk Along the River Spey

By ancient tradition, every three years the Queen of the West must cross the River Spey and walk its far bank to assert her sovereignty over the eastern boundary of her lands. The Spey marks where the Queen's territory ends and where the lands of other clans begin. This ritual is both ceremonial and deeply political.

For over eight hundred years, Clan Grant has been the Queen's bitter enemy. It began when the Grants betrayed Kiffan during the Viking invasions, a shame that has festered through the centuries. Both clans have nursed their hatred, each believing themselves wronged by the other, each carrying grudges that span generations.

When Annis arrived at the River Spey to perform the boundary walk, she brought four hundred soldiers, expecting confrontation. The Laird Grant met her with an equal force. Battle seemed inevitable.

The Miracle at Boat of Garten

Instead of fighting, Annis and the Laird Grant met in the middle of the river ford. In a brutally honest discussion, they confronted the true history of their hatred. Balgair, one of Annis's senior officers, confessed that fifty years earlier, the McRory clan had killed the Laird's grandmother, Lady Elise Grant, during a truce. He offered his own life in atonement.

The Laird Grant revealed a stunning truth: Lady Elise had taken poison and dressed as a messenger, intending to journey to the Queen of the West and give her life as penance for the Grant betrayal of Kiffan eight centuries before. The McRory axe that killed her had actually spared her from a slow and agonising death.

The Laird Grant, overcome with shame for his ancestors' ancient betrayal, knelt before Annis and offered her his sword and his absolute fealty. He called her 'My Queen' and offered her the prize of extending her sovereignty beyond the Spey for the first time in eight hundred years. Her wise head prevailed and she declined the opportunity, understanding that it might bring King James into conflict with her, compelling him to restrain any expansion.

At that precise moment, a great oak tree at the end of the meadow burst into flames. The mystical fire that had saved Kiffan the Defiant had returned. The Fire Tree burned for all to see, visible in sword reflections and in peripheral vision, a divine sign that the ancient power approved of the reconciliation.

Annis spared the Laird Grant's life and accepted his allegiance. The ancient feud was ended. The Laird Grant pledged to raise her a cavalry force for her eastern flank, something of which the Highland queen had dreamed her entire reign.

The Hidden Princess

Meanwhile, far from the River Spey, a young woman named Janine fled for her life. She had been working as a servant at Dunkeld Manor when a senior officer there dragged her to the cellars and tried to force himself on her. Janine heard bells, felt a strange calmness and lost consciousness. She woke to find the man brutally killed and lying in a pool of blood. When three men tried to attack her on the road, the same mysterious sequence happened: The sound of bells, a strange calm and lost consciousness. Again, she woke to find her foe viciously slain.

Exhausted and desperate, Janine was rescued by two kind-hearted brothers, Bruce and Brian, who brought her to Brech Woorlach, a grand mansion in the Lowlands. There, she met Francesca, who pretended to be a servant but who later revealed herself to be the daughter of the Duke and Duchess of Bo'Ness.

Janine believed herself to be the daughter of poor crofters, but possessed a beautifully crafted dragon ring that seemed far too fine for her humble station. Her mother had taught her to 'treat' her dark hair with a special lotion, claiming it prevented a family curse of baldness. In truth, it was a form of dye and when she stopped applying it, her hair turned out to be naturally golden blonde.

Janine felt strangely at home at Brech Woorlach. She could describe places in the grounds she had never consciously seen. When mystical flames began appearing on her hand and around the dragon ring she wore on a chain, Francesca and the others fell to their knees before her.

The truth was finally revealed: Janine had been brought to Brech Woorlach as an infant, hidden there for her protection during a time when traitors hunted anyone connected to the Queen's bloodline. Her hair had been dyed to hide her true identity, for all the Queens of the West were blonde. The dragon ring was one of the ancient symbols of the Queen's line.

Janine was not a crofter's daughter. She was born to greatness. She was the lost heir, connected by blood to the eight-hundred-year-old line of the Queens of the West. The flames that appeared around her were the same mystical fire that had saved Kiffan and appeared to Queen Annis at the River Spey, a sign that Janine, too, was chosen by the ancient power that guides Scotland's destiny.

The Brydda

The Brydda are an ancient people who have served the Queens of the West since the time of Kiffan herself. For them, service to the Queen is not merely a duty, it is a sacred calling, a faith passed down through generations. They believe the Queen embodies the spirit of Scotland itself, and they would die to protect her without hesitation.

Their loyalty is absolute and unshakeable, making them different from the feudal allegiances of other Highland clans. A Brydda soldier serves not because of clan ties or political advantage, but because they believe their Queen is divinely chosen.

The Shadow of War

Reconciliation comes at a price. As Annis stood triumphant at the River Spey, having achieved what no Queen before her had accomplished, warning horns sounded. The Clan Campbell had launched a coordinated attack from two directions simultaneously, striking at both the McRory camp and her new allies, the Grants.

The Campbells, who murdered Annis's mother seven years ago, had not forgotten their hatred. They saw the young Queen as vulnerable and the Grant alliance as a threat to them. They will not rest until she is dead.

The battle that followed was brutal and costly, leavings hundreds dead on all sides. Though Annis survived – saved by a miraculous intervention when an eagle fell from the sky to knock aside a spear meant to kill her – she was gravely wounded.

As she recovered from her injuries, the truth became clear: This was only the beginning. The Campbells would attack again, perhaps in days, perhaps in weeks, perhaps in months. They would come for her, as sure as night follows day.

And Now...

Queen Annis has forged a new alliance and has the prospect of a cavalry force on her eastern flank, but at the cost of making deadly enemies. Janine has discovered her true heritage but doesn't yet know her connection to the Queen. The mystical Fire Tree has appeared to both of them, marking them as chosen by the ancient power. And the Campbells are preparing their next strike.

The story of THE DRAGON RING begins here, as these threads begin to weave together and Scotland stands on the brink of a conflict that will determine not just who rules the Highlands, but the very fate of the kingdom itself.

CHAPTER 01

As Hamish Pottle and Alex Brennan stood in the dismal gloom of Coille Dorcha *(or 'Dark Forest'),* neither could deny the appropriateness of its name. Just being there sent a chill through their spines.

At the heart of the grim woodland lay the stronghouse of the Clan McCarthy, who presented themselves as *Torch Men* in the area – people meant to uphold some form of rudimentary Scottish justice in the area – but who were actually lawless thugs and robbers.

"Maybe this is all a dream and we are eventually going to wake up and have a laugh about it?" asked Alex Brennan in a whisper.

"My being an innkeeper is most certainly a reality," replied Hamish.

"How about me being a soldier returning from fighting in the front line of the Long War in Austria?"

"Yes, that rings true," Hamish whispered.

"I wish I were not keeping a watch on the road to Inverness for the man who murdered my sister."

"Aye, I wish we could change that."

"But what about your other guest?" Alex demanded, triumphantly, as he cupped a hand to the innkeeper's ear, "What about Constable Ewan Burberry, who is on a secret mission for King James and carrying a warrant of authority with a royal seal? Is that absurd enough for you?"

"It is absurd enough that he turned up at my inn with the dead body of the leader of the McCarthys slung over his horse," Hamish answered in a low voice, "But that makes it less absurd that the McCarthys have abducted him when he strayed too close to their hideout."

"But what is surely absurd enough to make this a dream is that he has an armed escort of thirty soldiers from the Lothian

Pikes and Muskets, sent by the king for his protection, but ends up wandering around alone?"

"The true absurdity is that we are both stupid enough to come here to try to rescue him!"

Turning to Alex, Hamish pointed to a McCarthy guard who was standing on watch in the distance and held a finger to his lips to urge silence. This prompt was completely unnecessary and, to emphasise the point, Alex contorted his face to imitate a dim-witted simpleton. Hamish ignored the mockery and walked his fingers slowly through the air in a pantomime of taking tiny steps, then pointed across to a dense clump of bushes.

The two men made their way to the chosen hiding place, treading with laborious caution. When they reached the spot, Hamish held up a flat palm for Alex to remain where he was and then made his way, stealthily, back to their horses. The innkeeper was hugely relieved that neither animal made any sound of greeting at his approach.

The McCarthy stretched his limbs and yawned at length, finally covering his mouth with his hand. It was clear that this man was feeling both tired and bored with his assignment. Within a few moments he yawned, again, then shook his head rapidly as if the action might throw out the fatigue.

Hamish came creeping back to Alex holding two bows and a quiver containing arrows.

"Musket fire would bring the rest of them running in a heartbeat," Hamish whispered, handing Alex one of the bows, "A blade would require us to get closer than we can with these twigs and leaves underfoot. An old-fashioned bow and arrow is silent and extremely deadly."

"I can land a musket ball in a thimble at fifty paces," Alex replied, "But landing an arrow on its target is another matter."

"Let's hope you are feeling inspired!"

"Let's hope he jumps into the path of my shot!" Alex countered.

"When we used to board an enemy ship in the dead of night," Hamish reminisced, in a hushed voice, "We'd climb our ropes or ladders as quiet as mice. Then we'd despatch the nearest guards by knife, the furthest with arrows, and the ones in between by whichever felt best."

Alex nodded, thoughtfully, while notching an arrow and giving the string a practice pull. He pursed his lips and wrinkled his nose in what seemed to be an assessment of his chances. After a couple more tugs, he nodded in reluctant approval and raised a slightly hesitant thumb.

The two men made their way a little closer to the McCarthy lookout, taking great care to step quietly. They approached within a distance of thirty paces before Hamish called a halt to their progress. They crouched in the undergrowth and both primed an arrow and drew back their bows.

The McCarthy watchman shuffled and stamped his feet to keep the blood flowing in them and periodically blew his breath into his cupped hands. Unaware of their presence, the man had not even the slightest idea that, for him, the sands of time in life's hourglass were about to run out.

Hamish's words were so quiet that Alex nearly didn't hear them. Almost like a dream, he became aware of Hamish counting down slowly from five. Alex forced himself to remain relaxed and struggled to prevent the tip of his arrow from wavering. Hamish reached the magic "zero" and both men let fly their arrows.

There was a swishing sound as the thin cord of cat gut on their bows eagerly sliced through the air, propelling the death towards their victim. The man stiffened, as if he had either heard the tell-tale sound or had experienced a momentary premonition. His head began to turn towards them. The speed of the arrows and the distance they needed to cover, cut short his reaction. He never saw their lethal approach nor from where they came. The two impacts, a moment apart, pushed him back against the trunk of the tree. From that position he slumped down into a heap at its base. A red patch was now forming through his tunic as the twin wounds gushed blood.

The two men crossed themselves, before muttering a blessing.

"Dear Lord, take into your care this soul, newly departed, and show mercy in your judgement as, one day, I beg you to show mercy to me."

They exchanged a look of half surprise at their near perfect synchronisation and promptly decided to prolong it.

"There…" said Hamish.

"But for…" responded Alex.

"The love of God…" said Hamish.

"Go I," Alex finished.

They exchanged a grim smile.

"So, was that a lucky shot, then?" Asked Hamish, turning to Alex with a quizzical look.

"You or me?" Alex quipped with a sly smile.

The two men laughed, then hurriedly thought better of it and looked guilty. They checked in all directions and were relieved that there was nobody to be seen. They made their way to where the dead McCarthy lay and dragged him into the bushes. There, they shielded him from view by putting leaves, twigs and branches over him.

Alex stood on the forest path and pointed the index fingers of both his hands in opposite directions and raised his eyebrows. Hamish shrugged, then, wagging his finger back and forth, indecisively, for a few seconds, picked a direction and jabbed his finger towards it. The two of them set off down the shallow gradient towards the point where the loop in the dirt track came around through the forest to approach the front of the McCarthy stronghouse. This was the trail they had abandoned, further back, in favour of coming up through the trees.

"I'm fairly sure they'll be watching the track," said Hamish, "Just in case anybody were either stupid enough or bold enough to follow it all the way round."

They made their way, instead, along the edge of the woods over rotting logs covered in thick moss and around partially felled trees that leaned precariously.

"You are right. It's unlikely he was the only one on watch," Alex remarked, "Do you have any idea how many of them there might be?"

"There were eight McCarthys in all," Hamish replied, "But – of course – their leader is nicely dead, thanks to Constable

Burberry, and now this one, too, so there are six of them left. This is presuming they don't have anybody else in cahoots with them."

They stopped on the brink of a saucer-like depression, liberally strewn with thorn bushes and nettles, and – thinking it too likely a place to lay a snare – they picked their way around the edge of it.

"If I had six men," Alex whispered, "Then I'd have at least three on watch out here, in the woods, and perhaps one watching close by the house. I wouldn't risk less than two in the house to watch a man the size of Burberry. They might just..."

Hamish suddenly put a finger to his lips for silence. Alex broke off speaking. Hamish moved the finger to behind his ear lobe and pushed it forwards in a gesture of straining to listen. Alex listened, too. There was the sound of water. It was not water cascading over rocks in a stream or a brook, it was more of a sustained fast trickle. It was as if somebody were emptying water from the spout of a can.

'*What?*' *Alex* mouthed, contorting his face in puzzlement.

Realisation dawned on the two of them at virtually the same time and Hamish made a motion as if drawing up his kilt with one hand while holding something out at pelvis height with the other. The sound they had heard was that of somebody emptying their bladder and the culprit was doing it up against a cluster of rocks, just ahead of them!

Hamish signalled for Alex to go round one side of the rocks. Whoever they were, they believed themselves to be alone. The noise of their sloshing and splashing urine was effective cover for Hamish and Alex to close in on them. Judging by its duration, the culprit had obviously been holding back for a long time and had only just allowed themself to succumb to the call of nature. Finally, the force of the jet of liquid began to wane and the unseen man gave a prolonged soft moan of relief.

'*Now!*' Hamish breathed, silently.

The moan abruptly turned into a gasp and then a whimper as Alex' arm came around the man's throat from behind and then forcefully up under his chin to keep his mouth closed. The man drove his elbow back, instinctively, aiming for his attacker's stomach or ribs. Alex, who had already turned to the side to avoid this possibility, pressed his hip against the man's lower back and lifted him onto his tiptoes. The elbow missed its mark. There was a thud as Hamish buried his dirk, up to its hilt, in the man's chest, straight through the heart. The man spasmed, his legs jerking rigid before going limp.

Alex released his grip on the McCarthy sentry and the lifeless body fell in a heap at Hamish's feet. The two men crossed themselves and paused to recite the words for his departed soul, before saying anything else.

"There is an even chance, heads or tails," Hamish announced, "That there is another one of them at a middle distance between us and the stronghouse. If not, just as you said, the rest of them will be either close to it or at the windows inside."

They dragged the corpse through the undergrowth to the edge of the gully.

"In truth, I hate and loathe men like these," announced Alex, contemptuously, as he hoisted the man's body off the ground by the arms and waited for Hamish to do the same with the feet, "Men who have lost all normal grasp of honour and who live their lives outside any bounds of decent behaviour. They are nothing more than wild animals."

"But a life is a life, nonetheless," Hamish declared, philosophically.

"Aye," Alex replied, in gloomy tones, "We are all God's children."

The two men swung the body back and forth a few times. As they did so, they counted each swing under their breaths. By the third swing they were happy with the momentum they had built up.

"After this!" Hamish urged.

They let go at the peak of the fourth swing. The corpse plummeted down through the overhanging greenery and smashed into the rocks of the basin below. Alex spat after the body, angrily.

"Would you have rather cut out his guts before we slung him? Or maybe done a full castration?" Enquired Hamish, slyly.

"Castration?" Asked Alex with sudden interest, "You wait till **now** to make that suggestion?"

Hamish suppressed a laugh and slapped him on his back.

"We can climb down and retrieve him, if you wish!" Hamish offered, with a wicked smile.

Alex rocked his head from side to side, pretending to be battling with indecision. After miming a pretence of beginning to climb down the steep drop, Alex laughed and slapped his own leg.

"If my arithmetic is not letting me down," said Hamish, "And the McCarthys have no reinforcements, then we have five of them left."

"I cannot imagine them to be the kind of men who will leave us many more opportunities to remain unscathed," Alex commented with a weary look of resignation.

"The McCarthys are well known in these parts. They are feared and hated in equal measure. The local laird tolerates them because it gives him an easy time," said Hamish, shaking his head in disgust, "The McCarthys do not allow dissent. Anybody who challenges them ends up dead. Anybody looking likely to challenge them is thoroughly beaten and, if they feel the need, they are left crippled for good measure."

"So far, then," Alex declared, "We have been lucky."

"Let's stay lucky!" Responded Hamish.

"Did you feel lucky when the first of those two mercenaries walked into your inn?" Alex asked, uncertainly.

"I recognised them for what they were," Hamish replied, "Men with no honour. This despite them having once been soldiers, from what I could tell."

"Taking down an axeman is no small feat," Alex noted, "The men who wield those things as their chosen weapon are known to be wickedly fast!"

"Aye, maybe they are," Hamish retorted, "But I am known to be wickedly wicked!"

"It's never a good idea to underestimate a man who can walk a straight line when the horizon and the deck beneath his feet are swaying side to side in opposite directions!" Alex replied, "Axe or no axe!"

The two men laughed and stood a while, mustering themselves for the task ahead. Presently, Hamish jerked his head in the direction of the dirt track.

"If I were them, I'd have somebody stationed where they could take an unhindered shot, from good cover, to pick off anybody following the trail," Hamish mused, rubbing his chin, "But I'm guessing that they have already put themselves in our position and acted smarter and less predictably that that."

"Much smarter!" Said a gruff voice, behind them.

Alex and Hamish froze and both of them began to raise their hands in the traditional pose of surrender.

"Put your hands onto your heads!" Barked the stranger, "Then kneel down."

"I'd rather die standing up, if that's okay with you," Hamish retorted.

"Oh, you'll die, for sure, but not just yet," their assailant assured them, "Now kneel down or I'll put a ball into the back of your head and talk to your friend, instead."

As they both dropped, reluctantly, to their knees, Alex and Hamish suddenly spun their heads to face each other and traded a look of surprise. They had, at the same moment, realised that it should have been impossible for them to kneel down without unslinging their muskets. As both now grasped, they had left the muskets in the long grass, nearby, when they had been disposing of the other McCarthy's body. Their minds tumbled and scrambled, trying to think straight.

"If either of you make a move," the stranger advised them in menacing tones, "I guarantee you it will be your last!"

With this, he pressed a pistol against the back of Hamish's head and, with his other hand, cut the strap holding Hamish's claymore. The big sword dropped to the forest floor with a thump.

"You, too," the man ordered, directing his voice to Alex.

Alex begrudgingly threw his claymore to the ground.

"Now," said the McCarthy, "Put the rest of your weapons on the ground behind you. Nice and slowly. Both of you."

Alex and Hamish pulled their pistols from their belts and extracted a dirk, each, from their upper clothing. They then both took another dirk from the top of their sock.

"I'm going to search the two of you," their captor announced, "And if I find any weapon on the one, I will shoot the other in the knee."

After a few moments' hesitation, a pair of brass knuckles, a donkey's hoof and another two dirks were produced and added to the pile of items on the ground.

"Go forward a measure," urged the man.

He waited for them both to obey before gathering up their weapons and folding them into a blanket. Once he had secured the blanket into a makeshift bundle, he let them get to their feet.

"Move along, up the hill," the McCarthy commanded, motioning with his pistol.

"If you'll show me just a little humanity, I am urgently needing to make water," Alex pleaded.

He and Hamish both tensed, deliberately not looking at each other, and tried not to hold their breath. This man's response would be crucial. He either did or did not know that they had just killed his kinsman. The man made a growling noise and appeared only to be annoyed.

"You can piss where you stand!" The man snarled, "You are not a woman, are you?"

Alex and Hamish were both hugely pleased to realise that this man had only crept up on them in the last minute and had not been observing them for any amount of time. They knew that, if he had been watching longer, there was a good likelihood that they would both be dead already.

"I have a sickness," Alex lied, feigning embarrassment, "And I am told my water smells bad. I'd not want you to catch a whiff of it and shoot me in anger!"

"Smell?" Hamish cried in a tone of outrage, picking up the other's lead, "One whiff of that foul poison and you'll want to throw up!"

Hamish made retching noises, "You'd do well to stand upwind of the filthy beast!" He added.

The McCarthy made a throaty noise of revulsion and kicked Alex in the backside, urging him towards the long grass. Alex raised his eyes to the Heavens and mouthed the words: 'Thank you!'.

"Be quick about it!" Demanded the McCarthy.

Alex pretended to stagger more than the kick truly justified and, still portraying a man unsteady on his feet, took a couple of steps into the tall, thin bladed grass. His mind spun like a child's whip-and-top as he struggled to think what to do. An absurd idea flashed into his mind and, almost before he could begin to process it, he was acting on it.

Alex gave a cry of strangled pain, startling both Hamish and the McCarthy, and took his hands from his head. His voice choked in his throat as he screamed in mortal anguish, stomping forward as if overbalancing.

"Bear trap!" Alex shrieked.

The McCarthy's face was a picture of consternation. He was pretty sure that no such device would be here, but, the uninterrupted cry of devastating pain seemed to sell him the deception or, at the very least, provoke an element of doubt.

Alex, having tumbled to the ground, now wrenched himself side to the side as if struggling against a tether. The McCarthy lowered his pistol in confusion. Sworn enemy or not, the idea of another human being having their leg in the vicious steel jaws of a bear trap was too distressing and agonising for instinct not to overcome caution.

The McCarthy began to step forward to look down into the grass at his prisoner's leg. His foot had hardly left the ground to take a second step before Hamish landed an almighty kick on the side of his knee. The blow, delivered with desperate force and urgency, resulted in a shockingly loud crack, like a stout branch being broken.

"Sorry!" Said Hamish.

The man crumpled sideways, his leg bending obscenely in the wrong direction. He screamed in pain. As the man toppled,

Alex lifted his "trapped" leg and drove his foot up into the man's groin employing all the power he could muster.

"Sorry, too!" Alex added.

There was another cry of pain and the man grunted as, with blotches of colour swimming before his eyes, he fought to not pass out. Suddenly, there was a flash of powder as he managed to fire his pistol. There was a billow of smoke and the barrel spat a flame as a streaking lead ball leapt out.

Alex would recall – telling the tale many times over in later life – that the projectile ambled its way casually towards him, as if out on a Sunday stroll. He remembered having a ridiculous amount of time to calculate its path, to push himself up from the ground using his shoulders, and then twist over to let the ball disappear harmlessly into the soil beneath him.

As the man hit the ground, Hamish dived and grabbed the bundle of weapons he had dropped. Forcing his hand into what served as its neck, he delved around and emerged – by pure chance – with the donkey's hoof. Hamish's face lit up with a malicious grin as he spotted the device. It was a leather bag, the size of a fist, that carried up to half a dozen lead balls. This was a devastating weapon in the right hands.

Hamish swung the donkey's hoof up in an arc, then immediately back down again, landing it against the head of the McCarthy. There was a sickening crunch and the side of the man's skull caved in above his ear. A red flash lit up the man's brain and his eyes superimposed it on his vision like a sparkling crimson fog. His ears rang with an impossibly shrill sound that caused him to convulse.

"I apologise," Hamish told him.

As their foe rolled to the side, barely clinging to the last shreds of consciousness, Alex hit him just above his left eye with the butt of one of the muskets.

"I apologise, too," he said.

The McCarthy saw a brilliant yellow flash of agony that pulsed and flickered madly in his vision. Abruptly, his world became soundless as an all-encompassing darkness enveloped him. It was a darkness that physically held him, like a giant fist. It was an eerie, ominous darkness that overwhelmed him with cold fear. It was a darkness from which he would never emerge. At least, not in this life.

CHAPTER 02

The nineteen-year-old Queen Annis, Queen of the West, listened to the eagles in the mountains as their calls and piercing cries echoed down the valley and across the plain. It was not hard to discern that they were pleased about something.

Annis smiled and wondered what kind of things made an eagle happy? The sight of a meadow full of rabbits? The discovery of swathes of ideal nesting material?

Annis, too, had reason to be pleased. She had encountered her Clan's long time enemy the Laird Grant, half way across the fording point on the River Spey near Boat of Garten. She had been there to perform the controversial ritual of walking the boundary of her territory on the opposite bank. The Laird Grant had brought an army of four hundred men and she a similar number. Despite this, not a single drop of blood had been shed.

She had been trained since childhood in the arts of war, for the Queens of the West had always been warriors first, but she was glad that there had been peace instead of battle.

She relished that the outcome of their encounter had been a miraculously benign one. Not only had they averted conflict, but – after a brutally frank discussion of the truly shameful history of their animosity – they had somehow managed to put their centuries long feud behind them.

In the end, the Laird Grant had pledged her his loyalty and had delighted her with the promise of the thing she had always dreamed of having: A cavalry on her eastern flank.

It had been at that very moment, to her complete astonishment, that the tree at the end of the long meadow had burst into flames. At first, only she and the Laid Grant could see it but, when she reached out and touched her two senior officers, they were able to see it too.

Annis slowly became aware of being watched and felt the gaze of Wild Flower – the Laird Grant's young seer and healer – resting on her. Wild Flower was a little girl who seemed to have a magical aura to her and some strange abilities. She was watching Annis with a look of joy.

The local priest – a man by the name of Father Blair – was only a few paces further away. Annis was amused to see Wild Flower make a discrete hand movement to invite the priest to join her. Father Blair's expression briefly flickered between something like annoyance and amusement. He was clearly unaccustomed to being summoned by a child, but he made his way across with only the merest glimmer of resentment.

"I want to ask you something," she confided.

Observing the conversation between the two, Annis was convinced that they were well familiar with each other. There was an unmistakable casualness and off-handedness and a strange informality. Their interactions, she had noted, were regularly punctuated by the priest looking exasperated. Talking with a little girl of no more than seven years old, who frequently spoke and acted like a woman of thirty, was blatantly challenging!

"Your Highness," said Father Blair, after long debate with Wild Flower, "It might be significant and extremely encouraging for your people if you were to consider observing a very old tradition practised by your ancestors."

"What tradition might that be?" She asked.

"In the old time, they would – periodically – come to the banks of the Spey and be publicly baptised, anew, in its waters."

"I have heard mention of this," Annis replied, flatly.

Annis did not feel comfortable, even yet, with being part of grand events like the one proposed. It was these kinds of formal ceremonies that made her miss her late mother, Queen Cydara, the most. They also had the effect of prompting her to compare herself, almost always unfavourably, with that wonderful woman.

The Clan Campbell had persuaded her mother to accept an Honour Guard, composed of their finest troops. Fearing that snubbing such a magnificent gesture would cause problems in the future, Queen Cydara had agreed, only to be murdered by them in an act of disgusting treachery. It was that betrayal that had thrust the crown on Annis' head, but not before the Campbells had tried their best to slay her, too!

Annis noted that Wild Flower was positively glowing with enthusiasm. Father Blair, too, was gleefully eager and expectant.

They looked, Annis thought, just like two little children who had woken up on Christmas Day and were waiting to hear if the forest fairy, Will O' the Nook, had called during the night with presents.

"Give me a moment, if you will?" Annis asked.

The unlikely pair nodded, vigorously.

Annis knew herself to be naturally gifted with a sword. Many a man in her camp, and many at the stronghouses of her many lairds, would testify to that!

Annis had taken many men by shock and surprise when she parried, slashed and attacked with unrelenting vigour and seemingly effortless skill. They had all quickly gone from "going easy on her" to mustering all they had just to survive. They, then, progressed to realising that they were completely outclassed.

She had always taken care to best her opponents in private. It was a very pleasing scenario, because it always played out the same. They would arrogantly presume that, as a woman and as a queen, she wanted to be avoid being publicly humiliated. In truth, it was *their* ego and vanity that she wanted to protect.

This kindly tactic proved to be a very productive one. When it dawned on her opponents that she had contrived to shield them from being humbled in front of others, their instinct was always one of gratitude. This gratitude would bind them to her with a ferocious loyalty.

Annis' mother had been proud of her daughter's sword craft and pleased with the consideration she exhibited towards the men she defeated. Her mother's good opinion of her was worth more to Annis than anything in the world.

Unbidden, Annis found her mother's words coming back to her and could hear her voice in her head, patiently and quietly instructing the future queen on her responsibilities.

'When you are a queen, you must act like a queen. People will have expectations of you.'

Annis wished that her mother were there, at that moment, to tell her what to do. Almost as if waiting for its cue, a curlew began its mournful cry across the meadow and, as if in derisory response, the crows in the gnarled trees by the water began a croaking reply. She recalled that her mother adored curlews. She would become almost spellbound by their haunting call and it would always bring a misty, far off look to her eyes. Annis often wondered if her mother were dreaming of her childhood.

Annis smiled at her recollections and noticed that, taking this as an encouraging sign, both the priest and Wild Flower seemed to immediately bubble with anticipation. She smiled more broadly and the two smiled back. The curlew sang its approval and the crows, as if in sudden reverence, allowed it to remain a strictly solo performance.

"Very well," said Annis, "Let us do this thing."

The priest clapped his hands gleefully and Wild Flower performed another elaborate and articulate curtsey, holding out an invisible skirt as she did so.

The Laird Grant gave Wild Flower a look of glowing congratulation. He was unmistakably pleased for this ritual to be happening on his land and almost swaggered as he gathered people together to make hasty arrangements. Father Blair retired to a tent that was thrown up at the edge of the field and changed into some more imposing robes and a pair of fine leather sandals that were happy to maintain constant contact with his feet.

Annis retired a little distance away to take the counsel of Balgair, the captain of her MacDonald Honour Guard and Gavin Crombie, her First Officer, who had been her mother's trusted advisor.

"This will please a lot of people," Gavin enthused, "It will please both those of high birth and the poor and humble, alike."

Balgair was equally positive.

"Word will spread far and wide and it will bring you great credit."

They young boy, Bobbins, who was the queen's unofficial squire, was sent back to the main body of her troupe with a message that her royal wagon was to be driven across for her to make herself ready and don her finery. Her personal maid, Morag, however, had other ideas and was unafraid to voice them.

"I do not think you should dress in your best attire, My Queen."

Annis immediately concurred.

"Very well, I will wear only the cotton garb that I wore under my armour. I will shun even the most drab of my silks, as wearing them would still risk conveying pride."

In a flash of inspiration, Annis changed out of her pure white cotton garb into a more ordinary pale cream cotton.

"This may not be the tawdry brown rough spun cloth of the poor but, as queen, it clearly expresses modesty without stooping to insult those who cannot afford any better."

Morag gestured towards the queen's wagon and, followed by the two young girls who were her helpers, Jet and Jade, she stepped up into it. Bobbins, not yet entirely comfortable around the two girls, hung around outside and made as if he were on guard.

Annis' transformation took little more than ten minutes. When she emerged from her wagon, Father Blair's face betrayed a little surprise. He had been unprepared for her total lack of splendour, but quickly recovered his poise. Wild Flower, however, was full of praise for her attire and told her so.

Bobbins took one look at his queen, put a hand over his heart and cried. Annis put her arms around him and hugged him. No words were required. Bobbins cried even more. Annis held him until he finally managed to stop crying and carefully dried his tears with the same tenderness as any mother. Still, neither said anything. After a little while, Bobbins took a deep, faltering breath and took a step away from her. Annis remained silent. Bobbins remained silent. Nobody present had any doubt that his loss of control was to be forgotten.

Jet and Jade looked pensive. Morag gently pushed them toward Annis, but they would not approach her. They were fearful that the boy had claimed their place in the queen's heart. Annis saw the pair and immediately understood the situation. She moved quickly to gather Jet and Jade into an embrace and they almost squealed with joy. They gratefully drank in the reassurance of her affection.

Annis move a little way away to gather herself, but found intrusive thoughts invading her mind. She knew herself to be the thirtieth of her line since Queen Kiffan, who had fought the Viking invaders. Yet lately, whispers had reached her ears. They told of rumours that there was another who claimed the title of Queen of the West.

The rumours, her advisors assured her, were Campbell lies, designed to sow discord. She had dismissed them. She had no option but to dismiss them because, if they were true... She pushed the thought away. She told herself that she must focus on the ceremony ahead.

Annis turned back to the little group of people around her and found all eyes fixed resolutely on the ground. She gave a little cough and they all looked up again.

Pointing towards the bank of the River Spey, Annis began to walk down to join the various parties who had assembled themselves downstream.   Everyone followed her.

At the river's edge, Annis declined the use of an ornate gilded cup to hold the baptismal water and insisted that a search be made for a more humble receptacle amongst the crowd. A crude, undecorated, metal drinking pot was found. The owner, a soldier, loaned it up eagerly. Wild Flower declared it to be an excellent choice.

"Your humility does you great credit, Your Highness," the priest declared.

"As does your love of these precious orphan children of ours," added Morag.

Annis smiled. They were, she reflected, something of a little family.

At the priest's bidding, Annis moved with him to the water's edge. With the assembled audience gathered in awed silence, she took off her sandals, made the sign of the cross, and stepped into the waters of the Spey. Turning to the priest, she lowered her head.

The priest began the ceremony in Gaelic but, half way through, opted to continue in Latin. At the appropriate moment, however, he resumed Gaelic so that all who were gathered could understand the words as he blessed her and poured the water over her head.

She knew, without a shadow of doubt, that the tall, old tree would be ablaze, but waited for an appropriate moment before lifting her gaze to view it for herself. To her amazement, there were three fully grown eagles circling the burning tree and, as she looked, they burst into a joyous, screeching chorus.

There was murmuring and discussion among the crowds that evidently endorsed the eagles as being a good omen. Christianity, it seemed, was unable to sap the appetite of the simple folk for the blessings of the ancient and mystic forces of the soil, the wind, the sky and the forests. These were evidently in full approval of their queen!

With a whooshing of wings, the three eagles wheeled across the meadow and suddenly appeared above the river bank. They gracefully swooped down to land on the sandy shoreline a few paces away from Annis and Father Blair. Several people cried out in surprise and more than a few drew back. Whatever the intention of these magnificent creatures, there was no doubt that they meant no harm.

For eight hundred years, high in the mountains, the lead eagle and its forebears had guarded something in their nest that their minds thought of as *'The Precious Thing'*. That task had been passed down from generation to generation. They had waited for the prophecy to be fulfilled. The prophecy about the girl with golden hair who would wear a hard white body shell and who would go down to the river with a big flock of her own creatures.

The largest of the birds had something in its beak and held it up high and wagged it side to side in a triumphant gesture that was eerily human. With very slow and purposeful steps, it approached Annis. Its demeanour was distinctly deferential and it bent its head low, fluttering its wings, as it reached her.

The huge bird stretched out its neck to bring its beak within arm's reach of the queen and seemed to be offering her the thing it held.

Annis held out her hand, palm upwards and, with painstaking delicacy, the eagle drew closer, still, and placed a small metal object into her hand.

The eagle looked at 'The Precious Thing' in her hand and made a soft cooing noise that sounded almost like crying. After hundreds and hundreds of years and after countless generations, the long wait was over. The prophecy was fulfilled. The deed was done.

"Dear God in Heaven!" Cried Father Blair, "I swear that this is an angel sent to us in feathered form!"

Word of this declaration rapidly travelled through the crowd and an approving muttering could be heard passing amongst them. Annis closed her hand over the object and felt its unexpected warmth. Her heart raced as she saw what this feathered envoy had delivered to her. It was a ring.

The eagle withdrew, moving backwards one step at a time, bobbing its head repeatedly as if an attendant at royal court. Once it was a reasonable distance away, it tested its wings, as if warning those gathered that it now needed the space to take off. The people closest to the bird moved back a few steps. The eagle studied the available space and appeared satisfied. With a few powerful strokes of its wings, it took to the air. Its two companions did the same, and the trio soared up into the sky with breathtaking grace. They circled once, then flew away towards the mountains, resuming their jubilant shrieking as they went. Immediately, the song of their fellows in the mountains rose to join them.

Annis opened her hand and gasped. There, resting in her palm, was a beautifully ornate ring. Annis' gasp turned into a sob as she saw the design. It was the head of a dragon. The ancient symbol of the Queen of the West.

Wild Flower was standing with her hands on her hips, nearby. Her face was decorated by an expression of delight and her lips with a knowing smile.

"It is the ring of the first of your line!" Wild Flower announced, "It was wrenched and cut from the finger of Kiffan the Defiant by a Viking, eight hundred years ago, leaving a wound like the figure three laid on its side."

Annis was amazed that Wild Flower knew exactly what the eagle had given her. She was most certainly too far away to be able to actually see the ring.

Annis looked at one of her own fingers and saw the familiar scar that was exactly the one Wild Flower had described. This, she was sure, was some kind of miracle!

"That ring," Wild Flower declared, "Was about to be stolen by the Vikings when an eagle snatched hold of it and flew away with it to the mountain tops."

Annis held the ring between thumb and forefinger and slid it onto the finger of her other hand. It fitted perfectly! She was astonished.

"Kiffan was once the greatest Queen of the West ever born," Wild Flower announced.

"She still is!" Annis cried, indignantly.

"No, Your Highness," said Wild Flower, dropping dramatically to her knees, "You are her equal."

Annis deliberately ignored her words and held up her hand with the ring facing the front. Wild Flower shuffled forward, still on her knees, and kissed the ring, fervently. Father Blair looked at the ring incredulously, as if he were afraid it would explode.

The Laird Grant approached, having no such qualms, and kissed both the queen's hand and the ring upon it. Balgair and Gavin followed in the same fashion. After them came Balgair's two lieutenants and then the group of senior escorts.

Annis held up her hand, again, to display the ring for the benefit of the crowd. The Grant army cheered, holding their weapons in the air and pumping them up and down in salute. Annis watched this gleeful tribute undulate in a rising and falling wave that surged back and forth across their ranks. It was, she thought, like watching the sea lifting and swelling over the rocks in a deep cove.

Annis noted that some of the local villagers had turned up. These local folks, who were stood to the side of the soldiers, were looking adoringly at her. Many had brought their children along with them. She was unsure whether they were from the territory to the West of the Spey, or had come from the Grant side of the river. Then, as her mind did a quick backflip, she realised that – to them, perhaps – they *were,* or had *become,* her people whichever side of the Spey they called home.

Annis motioned to Balgair and Gavin to approach her.

"It is my intention to go and greet the common folk," she told them.

Receiving approval from them both, she walked up the sand to the gaggle of villagers. As she came closer, they shrank back. It was apparent that close proximity to a queen filled them with unease. She smiled at them and a band of four small children, at their feet, wafted some tall reeds they had collected from the water as if they were greeting flags. Annis gave a little laugh at the spectacle and the children laughed back.

"Are they for me?" She asked.

In reply, the children began giggling and waved the reeds with increased enthusiasm. The adults with them appeared to relax a little but were plainly still anxious. A group of other small children had gathered up some small blue wild flowers and clutched them as posies. One of them stepped forward and held them out to Annis, not daring to come any closer.

One of the Grant soldiers raised a spiked baton and thrust it in the direction of the child.

"Stay there! Don't move!" The soldier shouted.

Annis looked at the soldier, calmly and coolly, then waved the child forward. With timid, uncertain steps, the child edged towards her. Annis crouched and the child came closer.

"Thank you. They are beautiful. I will treasure them," said Annis, taking the flowers.

The child squealed with joy and clapped her hands. Three other children came to her, the terror of their royal encounter now diminished, and handed her more flowers. The Queen of the West took them graciously, smelled them, smiled and then thanked each giver, individually.

"It's like in the Bible," Balgair confided, "Where the Messiah welcomes the children to him."

"I think she might regard that as blasphemy," Gavin warned.

Balgair looked offended, until the other broke into a grin.

"But we wouldn't care!" Gavin quipped.

The gathered crowd hummed with murmurs and whispers. While no individual words could be made out, there was a surge of good will and love so powerful that it felt as though it could be grasped in the air.

Queen Annis strode back to The Grant and his consorts and stood before them. The Grant bowed to her and those with him quickly did likewise.

"I am Annis, Queen of the West," she announced in a loud voice, addressing herself to the gathered crowd every bit as much as those who stood immediately before her, "I come from a line of Warrior Queens who stretch back for eight centuries. A line of queens who have never been slow to do the right thing and who have never held back whenever action was required."

Balgair, Gavin, Father Blair, Wild Flower, The Grant, his son and his close advisor all straightened and focused their attention on her, for they sensed that her mood had changed.

"I swear that I will serve The Highlands with all my strength and all of my heart," Annis told them, "I swear that I will serve its people, from the highest of them to the lowest of them. I swear that I will do this justly and fairly. I give you my word that I will never ask anyone to die in my name except that I would stand, with my sword in hand, and fight beside them!"

The roar that went up was absolutely deafening. All of those assembled cheered at the top of their voices. They roared their approval, they stamped their feet, they clapped their hands and they hooted loudly. The noise was so loud that she could feel it resonating in her chest.

CHAPTER 03

Annis' main camp was still back across the River Spey, up through the trees at the top of the bank. They heard, with great relief, the raucous sound of exultation for their queen and drank it in. They were grateful that they had not heard, instead, the horn to call them to battle nor seen the accompanying arrow trailing red and yellow streamers arcing high across the sky or the shrill cry of the whistle that would be tethered to its tail.

The anxiety and tension of the past few hours, awaiting possible bloodshed and death, was now replaced by euphoria. The rear guard of McRory troops cheered and clapped. The queen's assorted camp followers danced and hugged.

Sachairi, the Second-in-Command of the McRorys, shook his head vigorously as he saw various troops starting to unstrap their armour. He growled at them to stop and they all looked dismayed and annoyed. Sachairi remembered his father's saying and he barked it at them, now.

"Better to lose a cup of sweat in your armour than lose a bucket of blood because you are unprotected!" He scolded.

The soldiers grumbled and some of them cursed. A couple of the men, out of his sight, ventured a jeer. The Brydda soldiers, on the other hand, made no sound at all. None of them had ventured to take anything off. For them, service to the Queen of the West was more than a calling. It was a faith.

"You are soldiers first and you are farmers and crofters second," Sachairi told his troops, "Your swords are pledged to The MacDonald. Stand ready, stay prepared and make him proud."

The simmering resentment from a few seconds ago was instantly dispelled, as if pricking a bubble with a pin. The toll taken by constant waiting had frayed their nerves, but now clan pride had suddenly reinvigorated them.

Sachairi's face froze and his expression was slowly replaced by a dawning horror. As he cast his eye around the assembled troops, his look became still more disturbed.

"Where are the scouts?" Sachairi shouted, "They have not returned. They should have been back by now."

"Neither of them has come back!" Came a worried reply.

The entire camp was suddenly jolted by the realisation that they had overlooked the missing pair. They had been sent out an hour apart, the last one leaving a full hour ago. People looked round desperately, scanning through the faces in the crowded throng, trying to spot the missing pair. They could not be found.

As if responding to a cue, the sound of a single note, repeated in bursts of three, became audible in the distance. The thin, forlorn tooting carried an eerie edge of desperation.

Sachairi turned to one of his soldiers and made the action of pulling and letting loose an arrow into the air. The soldier's hand trembled as he notched the special arrow that signified an emergency. Drawing back the bow, he strained to apply his greatest possible strength. He held it for a moment, aiming high over the trees in the direction of the queen's party, and then let go. There was a swish and the long, thin needle of a missile hurtled up into the air. Easily clearing the trees, its wild flurry of red and yellow ribbons streamed out behind it. As it neared the top of its arc, the wind snatched out its tiny silver cargo and trailed it behind in its wake. They heard the thin, piercing screech of the whistle and their hearts lurched.

Far too soon to be a response to their own alarm, they heard the triple blips of a horn coming from the opposite bank of the Spey amongst the Grants. They had spotted an enemy on their own side of the river, too.

Sachairi felt his heart leap into his throat at the sudden realisation that whoever the enemy might be, they were mounting a deliberate and co-ordinated attack from two sides at once.

Ominously, the frantic horn, sounding in the distance from their scouts, stopped midway through a note.

CHAPTER 04

"I feel so strange," Janine confided, "I feel like I am in a dream. My life has been rushing at a fiercesome pace lately."

"You have every right to feel strange," replied Francesca, "For Brech Woorlach is a grand and imposing mansion and finding yourself here as our guest – especially after you had fled violence from your employer, carrying only a few things thrown into a pillowcase – you must give yourself time to adjust."

Janine gave her a weak smile, grateful for her sympathy.

"And," Francesca added, "Perhaps I have only added to your confusion by having posed as a servant, then revealed myself to be the daughter of the Duke and Duchess of Bo'ness who own Brech Woorlach."

"And sister to your two step brothers, Bruce and Brian, who so kindly picked me up in their carriage when they found me in a thoroughly bedraggled state by the side of the road."

"I am very pleased with them for that," Francesca beamed, "For you and your young companion…"

"The butcher's boy, Callum, who fled with me from Dunkeld Manor," Janine responded.

"For you and he," Francesca resumed, "Were in dire need of help and they, with their good hearts, provided it."

"You and your family took me in when I was desperate, showing me charity and kindness."

"Charity and kindness is a tradition at Brech Woorlach," Francesca declared, before suddenly looking sheepish, "But I regret having bored you witless, a few minutes ago, with my account of it and my family history. I even burdened you with how my great grandfather was shipwrecked, half dead, off the Western Isles and actually met the Queen of the West who tended his foul wounds with her own royal hands."

"You said 'The Queen of the West'?" Janine asked.

"Yes, you know of her?" Asked Francesca, looking hopeful.

"No," Janine lied, fighting to control her expression, "I just thought it sounded like a wonderful title!"

Francesca studied her and Janine hoped that she was not giving herself away by trying too hard to maintain control.

In truth, Janine had known about the Queen of the West from as far back as she could remember. Such a loyalty was a special part of Highland culture. It was the kind of thing that spurred Highland people to think of themselves as being from a different kind of place to the rest of Scotland.

If a line were drawn, from East to West from Perth through Crainlarich to Oban, it would mark the commonly accepted boundary between the Highlands and the Lowlands. Below that line, people who believed in the Queen of the West – if they were foolish enough to speak of it – were often viewed with suspicion. At worst, they were even regarded as traitors.

Janine was uncomfortable declaring herself a supporter of the Queen of the West. It felt dangerous to do so among people who were still relative strangers to her. There was no way that she could be sure that Francesca were not drawing information out of her to use, later, to trap her and accuse her. She liked these people, instinctively, but she felt that she didn't truly know them or they her.

A thought suddenly flashed into Janine's mind and she found herself voicing it before she realised.

"Who do people think I am, Francesca?" She blurted, "Who do they see when they look at me? They stare at me as if they have seen a ghost."

Francesca flinched as if she had been slapped and her eyes became troubled.

"They... They mistake you..." Francesca began uncertainly, "Because... Because you remind them of somebody, but..."

There was a soft knock at the door and Francesca called for the whoever was there to enter. Brian put his head around the door, as if unsure of his welcome. Janine clapped her hands in delight and he promptly stepped around the door, looking pleased. The expression of relief on Francesca's face, for the welcome interruption, was plain to see and Janine found herself inexplicably annoyed.

"Who do people think I am?" Janine asked, now directing her question at Brian, with no formalities or preparation, "Who is it that people think they see when they look at me?"

"Oh, yes!" Exclaimed Brian, remaining directly by the open door and looking sheepish, "I took a substantial reprimand from the duchess about that very thing, last night!"

Janine's face crumpled into a look of incomprehension.

"And from the duke, too!" Proclaimed the voice of Bruce, just the other side of the door, "He was not very pleased with either of us!"

Brian abruptly trotted a few steps forward in a comic stagger and Bruce emerged from behind him. It was clear that he had just playfully pushed his brother from the rear.

"We do not come empty handed," Bruce announced, scowling at his brother who was playfully holding up his empty hands to contradict him.

"We do," Brian corrected, "But our companion does not."

Callum made his entry, with perfect timing, dressed in a white shirt, a starched neckerchief, smart jacket and a formal MacDonald kilt.

"We have your manservant," said Bruce, triumphantly, his eyes twinkling at his little jest at the boy's age, "He brings food."

Callum drew behind him a tall wooden cart upon which were arranged several plates, of varying sizes, each with a bronzed steel dome over them.

"I have your breakfast, My Lady," said Callum, bowing deeply.

"Thank you," she replied, beaming at the former butcher's boy with a dazzling smile, "You are most kind and most considerate."

Her smile continued for a long moment as she studied the boy in his splendid new attire, but vanished in a heartbeat as she turned her eyes to the two brothers. The change in her demeanour was chilling.

"Who do people think I am?" she repeated, sternly.

"In that respect," Brian apologised, looking to his twin for confirmation, "We are complete buffoons!"

Bruce wrinkled his nose and crumpled his lips into a smile of clownish apology.

"We are *'clueless oafs, devoid of even basic wits'*, if the Duchess is to be believed!" Bruce moaned, feigning wounded feelings.

Janine, perplexed that nobody was actually answering her question, threw up her hands in despair. Grasping her own head by her hair, she pretended to shake it from side to side. Much to Janine's ire, Brian, Bruce and Francesca exchanged the kind of meaningful glances that only annoyed her still further. Callum, sensing the tension, excused himself and left the room.

The moment the door closed, Janine stamped her foot and all heads spun towards her.

"Who is it they see when they look at me?" Janine demanded, furiously, "Nobody has any true cause to know me, but they look at me as if they were seeing a phantom!"

The three looked wounded and Janine relented in her anger.

"I look out of that window," Janine confided, her sadness making her voice crack, "And I feel like I have come home after a long, long journey."

Janine stood, almost in a trance, and looked towards the window, lost in her thoughts.

"What's beyond the rise at the very top of the gardens?" Francesca asked, quietly.

"How would I know?" Janine snapped, with more hostility than she had intended.

The three said nothing and Francesca continued to survey Janine with her beautiful, kind eyes. Janine went to the window and looked out. She saw the long, wide lawn. She saw the fountain. She saw the ornate flower beds. She saw the line of weeping willows flanking either side of the vista as it stretched into the distance. She saw the shrubs and decorative hedging at the furthest end and watched as a peacock strutted out, imperiously, from one of the gaps and proceeded to fan out its magnificent tail.

Janine closed her eyes and didn't try to think. She just let her mind drift, as a clump of straw might tumble this way or that when caught in a breeze.

Without, at first, realising that she was doing it, Janine began speaking aloud.

"The land falls away down a shallow hill. As it levels out, there is a basin that forms a small pond. There's a statue in the middle. It is of a dragon."

"That's right!" Said Francesca, coming to stand beside her and squeezing her arm, encouragingly, "What sits beyond the pond?"

Without opening her eyes, Janine gave a doleful sigh, and spoke almost dreamily.

"There's a steep rocky rise with a cave cut into its base. The cut out forms a little chamber with a stone bench sculpted into its back wall. It's a quiet, peaceful place."

Francesca turned to Bruce and Brian and smiled warmly. The two brothers grimaced and their expressions made it clear that they disapproved of Francesca carrying on with this probing.

"What is above the cave?" Francesca asked, tentatively.

Janine frowned, knotting her eyebrows and thinking hard before answering.

"There's a flat platform cut into the stone, like a balcony, with a low stone wall across its front."

"When we were little," Francesca said forlornly, tears beginning to well in her eyes, "You and I used to spin the little sycamore seeds off the top of the balcony, to see who could get one to reach as far as the water…".

Bruce and Brian's faces dropped and they looked at each other fearfully, having realised the significance of what had just been said. Francesca caught their expressions and her eyes widened with sudden comprehension of her blunder.

Janine opened her eyes and looked at Francesca in a state of panic. The tension in the little group was electrifying and they all held their breath as they waited for Janine's reaction. Much to their relief, it quickly became clear that she had either not heard what had been said or had failed to absorb it.

"How can I have memories of things that never happened?" Janine asked, her voice almost a sob, her face grief-stricken.

"It's… It's…" Francesca began, reluctantly, hating that she had to lie to her childhood best friend, "It's just the shock and the upset of what you have been through," she said, the words tearing at her throat as if they were thorns, "And these new surroundings are playing tricks on your mind."

Janine looked, plaintively, at each of her companions in turn and they looked back with faces full of concern.

"I fear I might be losing my mind," Janine murmured, half to herself.

"No!" Said Francesca, very firmly, "That isn't it! Don't think that!"

"You might feel better after you've eaten something," Brian announced, "They will have started serving breakfast, by now."

Francesca whirled and glared at Brian and he visibly recoiled. He gulped and looked embarrassed at his lack of tact.

"There is nothing wrong with your mind," Brian intervened, having hurriedly recovered himself, "There are things that happen in this life that we simply cannot explain. I am absolutely certain that you need not worry about your sanity."

Bruce looked pointedly straight at Francesca.

"I am sure that everything you are experiencing will have a full and proper explanation in the end," his brother added.

Francesca cocked her head and glowered a warning at the two brothers.

"Perhaps," Brian suggested, "We could have some cakes brought up to your chamber."

"Yes, just so!" Bruce agreed, defiantly locking eyes with Francesca, "Run along, Francesca, and get her ladyship some cakes."

"And don't tarry about it!" Brian added, turning to hide his impish smile from Janine.

Francesca put both hands on her hips and thrust out her chin, looking daggers at the twins. Bruce and Brian faltered, at this, and looked at each other in confusion.

"Oh!" Bruce cried in sudden enlightenment, "I suspect that we may very well have not one but two ladyships in the room!"

"What?" Brian quipped, struggling to suppress a snigger, "You are no longer a maid, Francesca? Drat! I was just about to have you run and fetch my slippers while you were at it!"

Janine burst out laughing, her upset and confusion dispelled as if by magic. Francesca, delighted at the transformation, instantly deflated from her haughty stance and laughed, too.

The four of them stood in a little huddle, by the window, and the easiness and spontaneity of their bond made them unselfconscious about standing so physically close to each other. Bruce looked at Francesca, her face two hand spans from his own, and leaned forward and kissed her nose. She smiled. Brian looked at Janine, her face very close to his own, and – reaching up a finger – wiped a tear from the corner of her eye. In a flash he produced his handkerchief from the cuff of his shirt and offered it to her.

Janine took the handkerchief and looked at it, smiling, before holding it up as if a trophy.

"You gave me your handkerchief in the carriage, on the way here," Janine announced, "I felt so curiously and inexplicably relaxed and at my ease. So much so, that you managed to convince me to blow my nose."

They all gave a little laugh.

"Then, earlier this morning," Francesca confided, "You, Janine, had me blow mine on your own handkerchief and you made me feel unashamed to do so."

"So," Bruce quipped, unable to suppress a chuckle, "This is how we measure true friendship, now, is it? Blowing our noses?"

"Maybe it's magic!" Brian chirped.

"I promise I'm not a witch!" Janine protested, laughing and standing back from the group as if to give them safe distance from her.

"Upon my honour, she's not!" Said Francesca, holding up her hand as if she were a soldier swearing a military oath.

"It's the truth!" Janine insisted, adopting the same pose.

Seeing the expressions of her companions, Janine froze. They were all staring, open mouthed, at her hand. They were clearly shocked. She looked from one to the other and noticed, with increasing anxiety, that none of the three were looking at her face. All three were all staring fixedly at her hand. She became awkwardly aware that she had become immobile, stood like a statue, with her hand still held up.

"What is it?" Janine asked in a whisper.

Filled with dread, Janine slowly turned her head towards her hand, angling it towards her to better see its palm. What she saw made her yelp with alarm. There were flames!

She looked at the tongues of fire curling and spiralling like burning snakes on the palm of her hand. She parted her fingers and the red, orange and yellow pattern flickered across the gap, undulating and writhing. The faces of her audience had now turned to rapt fascination. Francesca, Brian and Bruce stared, wide eyed, at the swirling conflagration.

Janine was conscious that her hand felt no hotter than usual.

"There's no heat," she said in surprise.

Nobody answered and she quickly scolded herself for such a silly idea. How could she have thought that her hand might actually be on fire? No, this, she told herself, was a trick! Then, she promptly reconsidered. No, she decided, it was not a trick. Especially since the people who were the most likely culprits for playing a trick on her were far too amazed by it to be pretending.

Ever since she had been sent off into domestic service, Janine had become aware of having a gift for judging people's characters, moods and dispositions. She had become a personal maid far quicker than any of her peers. While, initially, this had spawned a little jealousy amongst some, it was short lived. Most people were happy for her. She was a good and loyal friend, who was almost always cheerful and who treated everyone kindly and with respect.

Her gift was now telling her that there had been a distinct shift in her three companions' moods and in the accompanying atmosphere in the room. They had progressed from initial wariness to nervous bafflement and then to a state of enchantment. Their gazes were those of people admiring a great work of art or an incredibly beautiful sunset.

"None of you are afraid," Janine declared, relieved that it had not sounded like an accusation.

Again, nobody answered.

Something in Janine's mind told her that the three had now become strangely comfortable with what they were seeing. She racked her brain for an explanation. The answer seemed to dangle excruciatingly out of reach. Then, in a flash, she knew! They had not ever been truly alarmed at what they were seeing. They had simply been astounded to see it happening right here and right now.

Janine was all at once filled with a mysterious sense of calm. She looked at her three friends and, after a little hesitation, they finally looked into her face.

"Where have you seen this before?" Janine asked Francesca, confident in her assumption.

Francesca looked surprised for a moment.

"I have only seen it once before," Francesca replied.

"But we," announced Bruce, picking up on the cue, "That is my brother and I, have seen it several times."

Janine looked at her hand, again, fascinated by the coiling tongues of flame. She reached with the index finger of her other hand and, with a little apprehension, she touched her palm in the midst of the fiery light. The flames immediately began to swirl around her fingertip like a tiny vortex.

"The last time we saw it," offered Brian, "Was with you in the carriage, on the way here."

"We saw flames light up the inside of the carriage," Bruce confessed, "But the source of the flames, which appeared to be just outside the window, simply did not exist!"

The three nodded in evident understanding of this strange apparition.

"When it happens," Francesca declared "There is a calmness and a tranquillity that is almost hypnotic."

Janine looked at her hand again, now content to leave the flames to perform by themselves.

"If I put my hand down, do they stop?" Janine asked, uncertainly.

"There are no rules," said Bruce, still captivated by the miniature inferno, "They have a life of their own."

Janine gave a little sigh, rendered almost desolate at the thought of extinguishing the flames, then asked the question that was scrabbling at the front of her mind to be asked.

"What do they mean?"

Bruce looked to Brian for inspiration, but he simply looked perplexed. Bruce' mouth contorted as he tried to frame the proper words and stopped as Francesca began to speak in his stead.

"They are like the lull before an incredibly beautiful storm," she began, in wistful tones, "They are like a faint glimmer of something spectacular and overwhelming that is forming in a place far away. Almost in another existence!"

"When was it that you saw this before?" Janine asked, resting her free hand gently on Francesca's arm for reassurance.

"When you stepped down from the coach, outside."

"I don't understand what they want with me," Janine frowned, "It just doesn't make any sense."

Brian spoke up, his voice blending reproach with both sympathy and pleading.

"Are you frightened by the flames, Janine?"

Janine looked at her hand, still swarming with tendrils of delicate flame and scoffed at the notion.

"No," she assured.

"Good," Brian said, looking pleased, "Because... This... This..."

Brian gasped in exasperation as the words he needed defied him and looked to the others for encouragement.

"It seems," Janine began, with undisguised weariness in her voice, "That none of you can actually speak to me without having a conference about it. If not a conference in words, then one conducted in looks, in gestures and in facial expressions!"

"That's because it's all so difficult," Bruce said, imploringly, "It's difficult to believe, difficult to explain and difficult to express."

Janine looked at her hand, again, now swathed in flames, and – still holding it up – very deliberately closed it into a fist. The flames promptly vacated her palm and began to shimmer on and around her clenched hand, instead.

"I don't know why this is happening to me. I'm just an insignificant nobody," Janine complained.

"No! No, you are not!" Francesca admonished, in furious indignation, "You were born to greatness!"

Janine looked at Francesca in shocked disbelief. Francesca's hand flew up to her own mouth in a flash and clamped solidly over it. Her eyes bulged with utter horror at the careless words she had just spoken. Bruce and Brian stood frozen to the spot, both looking startled.

Silent tears began to roll down Janine's cheeks and she held her arms wide towards Francesca. In an instant, Francesca leapt forward into her embrace and the two girls hugged as if their lives depended on it.

"All the children here are orphans," Francesca said, when she had recovered her voice, "They tell me their dearest secrets. They all dream who their parents might be. They make up all kinds of things. They dream that they are born of noble parents who, one day, will come to claim them and shower them with wealth."

Grasping Francesca by her shoulders, Janine, eased her away until she was at arm's length, and looked at her quizzically.

"Even as a small child, it broke my heart to be the daughter of a duke and duchess and to hear the misery of these children," Francesca told her, looking meek and apologetic, "I used to get out of my bed, every night, and creep downstairs to sleep with the children we had taken in. My governess used to take me back up to my bedroom, at first. Eventually, my parents accepted that I could not tolerate the sumptuous splendour of my own bedroom and that sleeping in the crowded dormitory was my choice."

Janine nodded and drew her friend close to resume their embrace.

"I remember the night that you arrived, Janine," Francesca confessed, "I remember it as clearly and as vividly as if it had happened just yesterday."

Janine propelled Francesca back to arm's length, again, this time with considerably less gentleness and looked at her with shock and hurt in her eyes.

"I'm not an orphan!" Janine protested, the edge to her voice harsher than she had meant it to be, "I have a mother! I have a father! I grew up with them!"

Francesca rested her hands on Janine's own and squeezed them in response.

"It was different with you," Francesca said, "You came here, that night, not because you were abandoned or homeless, but for safety and protection."

"For safety and protection?"

"You were in danger. There were people – at that time – hunting down those they supposed to be traitors to the king. They came to where you lived, but you were rescued, just in time."

"I have nothing but contempt for anyone who could harm a child!" Exclaimed Janine.

"You have to believe me when I say that these people were evil!" Francesca appealed, "These people were vicious, unprincipled animals! They were, themselves, traitors! Traitors to Scotland!"

Janine stared in fascination into Francesca's beautiful face, now transformed by her words into one lit with fury, venom and hatred. Janine gave a little shudder. Brian quickly interrupted, placing a hand on either girl's shoulder.

"They were looking for somebody in particular," Brian advised, "And, tragically, there was a fear that they might mistake you for that person."

Janine looked at Brian in complete puzzlement. Francesca fought an overwhelming urge not to look at Brian. The casual ease of his lie had caught her off guard.

"Even as a child," Brian continued, embellishing his deception, "They might have mistaken you for their quarry. In fact, to be honest, it would have been because you were a child."

Francesca watched Janine's face as it fell still while her mind furiously worked through this information. It was as if a thousand cogs were spinning and whirring in a complex machine! Suddenly, her attention returned.

"Who did they think I might be?" Janine demanded.

"The future of Scotland," Brian replied, honestly.

Janine's astounded expression was exquisite.

"There are people who believe in fairy stories," Bruce interjected, "And who have voracious appetites for intrigue, rumour and scandal. A group of such people, back then, got a ridiculous idea into their heads and started causing trouble and upset all over Scotland. Nobody was really safe from their stupidity."

Janine looked sceptical and unconvinced.

"You and I were less than two years old," Francesca announced, eager to steer Janine away from her line of questioning, "And, the nursery matron told me, when you arrived – which was during the night – that I stood up in my cot, holding on to the rails, and wouldn't go back to sleep until I was incapable of standing any longer due to fatigue."

Janine looked perplexed and bewildered and began to question her own sanity.

"How can these things have happened if I don't remember them?" Janine asked, choking back her tears, "This is another person you are speaking about!"

Janine's lip trembled and she looked at her new friends beseechingly. The two brothers moved either side of her and the trio wrapped their arms around her, in unison, and hugged her.

"Not another person," Francesca cooed soothingly, "Just another life."

"If you remembered nothing of this place," Bruce said, gently and reassuringly, "We would have said nothing to you, but each of us has seen the way you stop and look around, distracted and disorientated, yet on the brink of recognition."

"We've seen you stare through the window in confusion," Brian added.

"Confusion is all I know!" Janine replied, sounding utterly dejected.

"Just look at your pretty hair, though!" Said Francesca, examining it and tracing her finger across the hairline on Janine's forehead.

"Pretty? It isn't pretty! My scalp has an affliction. I need to treat it, regularly, with a remedy that my mother showed me how to make," Janine revealed, "If I didn't use it, then my hair would all fall out, just the way it happened to my mother and my grandmother and her mother before her. The women in my family are cursed by it."

"You treat your eyebrows the same way?" Francesca asked.

"Why, yes, I do!" Janine replied in surprise.

Janine's expression dropped as she took offence at the glimmer of amusement in her friend's eyes and the smile she was fighting to suppress. Seeing the change of expression, Francesca quickly reached up and inclined Janine's head to kiss her hair.

"Oh, how I envied you when we were small!" Francesca confessed, "You and your beautiful, shining golden hair!"

Janine looked horrified.

"I have dark hair!" She protested.

"The curse of which you speak," replied Francesca, "Has truly afflicted your family for generations, but it is nothing sinister."

Janine was now dumbstruck.

"The serum you use," Francesca advised, "Is of no medical worth. It is not to treat your scalp. It is merely hair dye."

Janine grabbed at her own hair, as if it were about to fly off her head, and looked at it in disbelief.

"Everything that has happened to you in your life has been for a reason," Brian declared, "It has been to keep you safe. We here, in this house, are sworn to protect you."

"We did not know you when we were in the coach," Bruce explained, apologetically, "Because something beyond our comprehension did not allow us to recognise you. That something is a force of unimaginable power that can do anything it wishes."

"But," Brian interjected, "That force exists only by the Will of God. He enables and permits it to be. He authenticates it by sending a sign. The sign of fire. The sign that God has used – since time began – to communicate with his people."

Janine looked to her hand, which she had lowered, and felt a twinge of disappointment on seeing that there were no longer any flames. Without knowing why, she found herself looking down. When she did, she saw tiny fluttering tendrils of flame dancing on her blouse, between her breasts. She instinctively reached for her own throat and felt the chain around her neck tingling and vibrating. Slowly and with infinite care, she pulled up the chain and her mother's dragon ring swung out, wreathed in a shimmering aura of fire.

On seeing it, Francesca dropped to her knees and bowed her head in deference. Bruce and Brian quickly knelt, too, lowering their heads in the same pose. Janine stared at them, blankly, her mind fighting to make sense of it.

Suddenly, a voice came from the doorway behind them and she turned to identify the speaker.

"It is time," the Duchess of Bo'Ness announced, "In fact, it is long past time, that you were reacquainted with a certain someone."

Janine began to curtsey but, at the first glimpse of the motion, the duchess held up her hand for her to stop and, instead, curtsied herself.

"Who am I?" Janine begged.

"If you would be so gracious as to follow me, I will take you to the person who can explain everything," the Duchess replied, pushing open the door and stepping back outside into the corridor.

CHAPTER 05

Alex and Hamish stood poised, holding either end of the latest McCarthy corpse, in readiness to swing it over the edge and down to the bottom of the gully to join its kinsman.

"If fate is being kind to us," said Hamish, "This leaves four of them."

"That would be four very dangerous men," Alex replied

"I have a very bad feeling that Will O' the Nook is playing games with us!" Hamish confessed, beginning the first swing of the corpse to build up momentum, "Things are going far too well for us."

"That or he hates the McCarthys!" Alex mused, grunting under the exertion of the next swing.

"Or we are blessed!" Hamish mused as he stepped forward into the final swing.

Together, they released the body to plummet sixty paces straight down onto the rocky outcrop below. It clattered through the branches and unruly bracken as it fell, smashing its way to its final resting place, and came to a halt in a crumpled heap.

The two stood in silence for a few moments as they watched the undergrowth sway and wobble before settling to leave no trace of the newest resident's arrival. The two men crossed themselves, in almost perfect synchronisation, and said the words for the newly dead.

After a short while, as if by unspoken agreement, they moved away from the edge. They gathered up their weapons, including the pistol their attacker had dropped, and recovered the things that had become scattered during the struggle. Presently, they made their way back to the path that led in the direction of the McCarthy stronghouse.

"Blessed?" Asked Alex, as if no time had passed since it were mentioned.

"Aye," Hamish confirmed.

There was a long pause.

"Blessed?" Alex repeated, with more emphasis.

"Aye," Hamish replied, "That's what I said."

"Blessed!" Alex mused, toying with the word as if it were a strange and novel concept.

They trudged down to the joining point with the track and – without debate – began to make their way up the shallow rise that skirted the forest in a long arc. Neither man spoke, their silence lasting several minutes.

"Blessed," said Alex, eventually, in a despondent tone.

Hamish came to an abrupt halt and stood still. Alex stopped, too, and looked at him impassively. Hamish shook his head, wearily, as if resigning himself to commencing a tiresome chore.

"Sailors are superstitious," Hamish began, "And believe things, a day out from shore, that they would scoff at if they had dry land beneath their boots."

Alex cast a glance at Hamish and nodded in acceptance.

"Even men who weigh almost as much as an ox and who are built very much the same as one," Hamish continued, "Can fall prey to fanciful ideas when they let themselves. I have been becalmed at sea, with not a breath of wind to drive us, floating motionless on what looked like a mill pond, and I have seen men's minds turn to fanciful nonsense and superstition."

The two resumed walking, keeping a sharp eye open for sentries, and Alex grunted his agreement.

"The same is true in the forest," Hamish continued, "If you sit still and drink in the quiet and the feeling of the place, you can start to believe the most extraordinary things. When it's midnight and you are low on fuel for your fire, Will O' the Nook becomes less of a children's story and more of an eerie possibility."

Hamish did not have to see the smile on Alex' face to know that it was there.

"There are myths and there are legends," Hamish went on, silently pointing out a trip wire across their path, "And it's a foolish person who would disregard them as having no kernel of truth."

The two men stopped and both took great care to step over the trip wire.

They had hardly gone another five paces before Alex, this time, discovered another trip wire. This particular trip wire was linked to a cluster of metal cans that dangled from a nearby branch. They had a wordless, animated discussion as to the merits of different routes and agreed that they were intended to change their path and, therefore, they didn't.

Hamish urged that they remain silent and waited for a full minute before he was satisfied that nobody could hear them.

They reached the top of the rise and cautiously surveyed the undergrowth for further traps and wires. The enemy would surely believe that they would try for deeper cover within sight of the stronghouse, so they remained by the edge of the track, instead.

"I don't think any of the three of us – you, me or the constable – have crossed paths for no reason at all," Hamish announced, "Whether fate or destiny exist or not, I believe we are meant to be here."

"I feel the same," replied Alex.

"Sometimes we are called to a task and, in doing so, we are blessed."

"To be frank," Alex replied, "We don't know if there are other people who are being drawn together in other places, right now, but what is happening is definitely something that is meant to be."

Hamish nodded, seriously, both happy and relieved to hear of the other's like-mindedness.

"My father believed in legends and he was a wise man and nobody's fool," Hamish avowed, "He said that there is a time when all the things that are needed will come about and happen. He said it is called 'The Quickening'."

Alex looked thoughtful for a moment before nodding, contemplation written large across his face.

"The Quickening," Alex mused, almost to himself.

Hamish gave a little grunt and shot Alex a warning look.

"If you start repeating that word over and over, Alex, like you did 'blessed', I'm sorry to say that I'm going to have to punch you on the nose!"

The two friends laughed soundlessly and pretended to spar, trading ludicrously clumsy punches like a couple of drunkenly incompetent boxers. Once their amusement with this charade had finally waned, they crossed over the dirt track into the sparser forest and made their way through the trees.

They were fairly certain that the route they were taking would be the least expected one. Their wisdom was confirmed by finding no more trip wires or traps waiting for them until they were a hundred paces from the McCarthy stronghouse. Hamish promptly declared the new device they had found to be suspiciously too easy to spot. The pair spent several minutes carefully prodding and probing around in the vicinity before finding two more well concealed trip wires a little way either side of the decoy.

Hamish and Alex installed themselves into a thick bramble hedge. They judged it to be reassuringly too sharp, dense and aggressive for any sane person to have intruded into it to lay snares. From this spot they silently watched the stronghouse for fifteen or twenty minutes before backing out of it to talk in the dense thicket beyond.

"It's almost as if nobody is in there," Alex declared.

"Aye," replied Hamish, "It's almost like an open invitation."

"But they wouldn't have had lookouts posted around if they really weren't there, would they?" Alex asked in puzzlement.

Hamish, deep in thought, didn't reply for a while, his face creased in concentration and his gaze distant and unfocused.

"Something is definitely wrong," Hamish announced, "But I am worried that they may purposely mean us to think that. It could be some kind of ruse to throw us awry."

"It's like flipping a coin," Alex observed playfully, "It comes down heads or heels. One way we win. One way we lose."

Hamish gave him a scornful look.

"All I'm saying," Alex retorted, "Is that every decision we make is good or bad and we can never know the outcome when we make it."

Hamish made a disgruntled rumbling noise in his throat and didn't venture to comment.

"So far," Alex continued, still determined to make some kind of a point, "We have been almost too lucky."

"Lucky?" Hamish repeated, indignantly, "We've been lucky?"

Alex pulled in his chin by moving his head back until his chin scarcely overhung his neck. This exaggerated gesture of wariness was answered by raised eyebrows from Hamish.

"You came back from Austria, alive and well, simply because the odds were good?" Hamish challenged, "You learned about the constable, back in Perth, by the whim of chance? You happened upon my inn by a fluke? The constable just so happened to walk in through its doors by sheer good fortune?. You came here and then this situation arose by nothing more than coincidence?"

Alex looked troubled. Hamish fumed. After a long minute of silence, Hamish spoke. His voice, once more, calm and unruffled.

"The tree in your dreams burns as a sign," Hamish declared in hushed tones.

Alex recoiled, looking aghast, as his eyes sprang wide in disbelief.

"How could you know about that?" He cried.

"I have felt it." Hamish replied, "I have seen its flames on my wall as I hover on the brink of sleep. I know my wife has seen it, too."

Alex had an expression of shock on his features and was too dumbfounded by Hamish's disclosure to try to hide it. He opened his mouth to speak, but none of his words would venture onto his tongue.

"It's the Quickening!" Hamish said with a tone that brooked no argument.

Alex blinked and held the innkeeper in a suspicious gaze, still fearing that he had simply misheard him.

"The tree?" Alex asked, blankly.

"Yes. The tree."

"Have you heard the sound of the tree alight?"

"Yes. It crackles and roars."

"It does!" Alex replied in awe, "It does, indeed!"

"I started to see and hear it in my dreams the day you arrived at the inn," Hamish insisted.

Alex nodded, slowly. He was clearly now only present in body, his mind having travelled elsewhere.

"My grandfather believed in magic," Alex confessed, "He believed that it was the lasting influence of the angels, from when they used to live on the Earth, before they were summoned by God to return to Heaven."

"My father," Hamish revealed, "Believed that there was Black Magic sponsored by Satan and White Magic sponsored by the angels. He believed that our lives were influenced by both sides, one constantly attempting to lead us astray and the other to our salvation."

Alex slowly turned to Hamish, his previously wavering look now having become determined. His shoulders had lost their slump and his head was now held high. He looked deliberately at the Italian hunting musket laying on the ground, nearby, and then back at Hamish.

"We have a job to do," he said.

With slow, deliberate care, Alex picked up the weapon and took a pin from his belt and used it to extract the cotton bung from the end of its barrel. Next, he rotated the sparking drum, using the pin as an improvised pick, he scratched and roughened it's visible surface.

Hamish watched, warily, unsure of what to say or do.

Alex took off his neckerchief and, unfolding it to expose a clean, dry portion of the material, began to dab it against all of the musket's components to ensure that they were completely dry.

Next, he did the same with his pistol. Working efficiently, but without hurry, he methodically prepared that weapon for firing, too. Finally, he produced the pistol he had taken from the body of one of the McCarthys and repeated the process with that, as well, until he was satisfied.

Hamish could no longer restrain himself and cleared his throat to draw the other's attention. Alex ignored him and continued to busy himself by rechecking all three firearms. Hamish cleared his throat, again, and Alex looked up, impatiently, and made a resentful rumbling in his throat.

"What are you doing?" Hamish asked, instantly regretting such an idiotic question.

"I'm either skinning a rabbit or I'm making these ready to fire. Would you like to take a guess which it might be?"

Hamish grimaced but didn't grace the other's sarcasm with a reply. After a few moments, Alex grunted his annoyance and looked straight at his companion.

"I'm going to do what we came here to do," Alex said in a more measured tone, "I'm going to set about finding out if the McCarthys have the constable."

"There are only two of us," Hamish protested, indignantly, "And we don't know for certain how many of our enemy there might be."

"There are none so zealous as those who have converted from another faith," Alex proclaimed, quoting his grandfather.

Hamish looked blank and knitted his brows. In truth, he had not quite known what he would do once they reached the McCarthy stronghouse, but Alex' certainty made him nervous.

"You have convinced me," Alex said with only the vaguest flicker of a smirk, "That what we are experiencing is The Quickening. I believe it is true. I believe that what is happening to us is, indeed, that very thing."

Hamish looked at him dubiously, employing the kind of pained expression usually reserved for wandering beggars who claimed to be a king.

"And?" Asked Hamish, urging him to carry on.

"I'm going to run over to that house. I'm going to smash through those front windows. I'm going to hurl myself inside. I'm going to shoot as many McCarthys, or their collaborators, as I can before they kill me."

"Will they not shoot the constable as soon as they hear you breaking in?"

"If they were of a mind to kill him," Alex chided, "Then I think he would be dead already."

Hamish looked on, only partially convinced.

"If they have kept him alive," Alex reasoned, "Then they are either intending to take him and present him to somebody with authority or hold him while that person comes here."

Hamish rubbed his chin, ruminating on the possibilities, but – before he could reply – Alex interrupted him with a question.

"How is it even possible that you knew I was dreaming of a tree on fire?" Alex asked.

"I saw it. I saw it on the walls. I knew for certain."

"Even though that would be simply impossible?" Alex countered.

"Yes," Hamish replied meekly.

"This situation is exactly the same," Alex announced, "I know that we need to rush at their stronghouse. I know with absolute certainty."

"Even though there are only two of us?"

"There won't be only two of us."

"Alex, there's you and there's me."

"I have been here, before, in my dreams," Alex announced, "This feels oddly familiar."

"Déjà vu?"

"You know about that?"

"I may only an innkeeper, Alex, but…"

"But you are not stupid."

"I was a sailor, for many a year, and I have read more books that I would ever care to count. When you are at sea, there is little else to do, other than get drunk. There is no subject that you'll not read about if you are sufficiently bored!"

"Is that an answer?"

"It might be."

"We have something to do, Hamish, and we need to do it."

Alex looked at Hamish, calmly and solemnly, without speaking. For a long few seconds, Hamish did not respond. In the end Hamish groaned and, bending with elaborate and exaggerated deliberateness, he took hold of his hunting musket and set about preparing it.

After checking the mechanism and drying the firing surfaces with the corner of his cuff, he propped it against his leg. Next, he took two pistols out of his satchel, one his own and one taken from a dead McCarthy. After carefully checking them for readiness, he slipped them both into his belt, one either side.

"Right," Hamish said, with grim resignation, "Are you ready to die?"

"I have been ready to die ever since I escaped death for the first time," Alex declared.

Hamish held the other's gaze for a moment, in sad contemplation, then nodded his sullen agreement with the sentiment. Being alive during adversity had a cost. The cost was dogged determination and unrelenting slog. He was weary to his bones from paying that cost.

"Five years ago, I held my daughter in my arms while she died," the innkeeper announced, grimly, "Then three years later, I held her brother as he died."

Hamish kicked at the soil, digging the toe of his boot into it and lifting a clump of it into the air.

"The call of this cold, damp ground holds no fear for me."

With this, Hamish stamped his heel into the hollow he'd created, as if daring it to respond.

"I'll tell you this, Alex, I'd just like the pleasure of taking as many of those McCarthy's with me as I possibly can when the time comes!"

Alex stood his tallest and took in a lung full of air before letting it out slowly, a vague hint of steam from his breath forming in front of him as the temperature around them continued to drop.

"You are never quite so completely and utterly alive as you are just before risking death," Alex said, nostalgically.

"Nor, often times, so numb and disorientated from fear, either."

"Even the most senseless, boring, backbreaking tasks are suddenly to be envied. Working your fingers to the bone seems to be a stroke of good fortune compared to the prospect of kicking and flailing your last moments in a pool of your own blood, piss and shit!"

The two men laughed, suppressing the volume of it, but without impairing the intensity of the joy at their camaraderie.

"The shit was always the worst part, of course!" Quipped Hamish, leaning forward confidingly, "Fear is fear and its effect is pretty routine!"

Alex looked intrigued and a question seemed to flash across his face, but he held back from asking it. Hamish answered it, none-the-less.

"Aye!" Chortled Hamish, his smile widening as he recollected events, "It happened to me a couple of times! In my earlier seafaring days, of course!"

Alex laughed, as quietly as he could.

"Believe me," Hamish declared, "Another ship crashing up against the side of your own in preparation to board you and take you by force is a scary business! When a huge mass of screaming pirates pours onto your deck – leaping off ladders, sliding down ropes and climbing across planks – you'll find that fouling your britches is as natural a reaction as you are ever likely to encounter!"

"I know it," Alex replied, laughing quietly, "It happened to me, once! It has also happened to more people around me than the average person would ever imagine!"

"War is an ugly business," Hamish affirmed.

The two men stood in silence for a little while, the need for words exhausted. Eventually, they looked about, systematically scanning their surroundings and listening carefully and attentively for noises. They studied every possible location for shelter or cover that an enemy might use to hide.

Hamish leaned forward and brought his mouth close to Alex' ear to whisper to him.

"I have an odd idea that we are not alone," said Hamish, "But I can say with certainty that it's not any of the McCarthys or their gang around us."

"I cannot see anybody and I don't hear anybody," Alex concurred, "But I, too, have the strangest feeling that we are being watched."

Hamish pointed in the air above them.

"The birds are quiet in the branches over our heads," he said, "Just like you would expect them to be with us below them. If you listen, you can hear them further in the distance, but there are two groups of trees fairly near to us, and there isn't a sound from the branches of either one."

"It's possible that we are wrong and that our minds are just playing tricks on us," Alex said, trying to keep his voice as low as possible.

"Yes," Hamish responded, taking another look around them, "It's possible, but it's unlikely."

Alex picked up the hunting musket that leant up against his leg and positioned it with the barrel supported by one hand and the stock by the other. He looked to Hamish as he slipped his hand over the trigger guard. Then, his finger slowly moved to nestle against the trigger. Hamish said nothing, but took up his own musket and, calmly and unhurriedly, gripped it in a similar fashion to his friend.

The moment had come to act. It was time to attack their enemy.

"The least likely thing they would ever think we would do," Alex announced, "Is to come in through the front windows. So that is what we will do, as it will deliver the most surprise."

"The shutters are open so that they can see out," Hamish observed, "And the bars, may — if we are lucky — yield to a few really good, hefty kicks."

Hamish held up his crossed fingers to signal it to be a fervent wish.

"Either way," Alex replied, "We can fire into the house once we break the glass and the constable, unless he is chained in a standing position, will be getting flat on the floor at the first sign of our assault."

The two men stretched and flexed to ensure that the bows they had hung from their backs did not hamper their movements and began to cautiously move out from cover.

All at once a sudden flash of light hit their eyes. It lasted for a single second and then was gone. Almost immediately, it was back, again. It endured for only a brief moment, before it ceased. A second later, there was another flash.

Hamish tapped Alex on the arm and pointed towards the origin of the light. Over by a vegetable patch, next to the fortified house, was a group of mirrors hanging from strings. Next to the mirrors were some bells and a couple of metal tubes. These devices were clearly designed to reflect the sun or make a noise when the wind blew. They were, they realised, no more than simple bird-scares.

"The sun is behind the clouds," Hamish whispered, "What light is bouncing off those mirrors?"

The mirrors seemed to have their own mysterious source of light. As they continued to twist and rotate, the yellow, orange and red flashes became brighter. Alex and Hamish exchanged a glance as they both realised that this was a reflection of fire.

"It's fire," replied Alex, quietly, "But there is nothing, anywhere, that is aflame."

This was blatantly true, for even the briefest look around confirmed that there was absolutely no fire to be seen in any direction. It was as if the flames were being generated in the glass itself. This, they knew, was impossible. Alex and Hamish looked at each other, again. This time they shared a feeling of inexplicable confidence and reassurance.

"It is time," said Alex, taking a deep breath.

A moment later, he set off at a slow trot, building up to a run. As he went he heard Hamish running behind him. Alex looked ahead to the window and there was nobody visible. He looked briefly down at his feet, taking care not to stumble in his haste, and lengthened his stride.

Alex and Hamish both flinched as a piercing, high-pitched whistle sounded, splitting the air and ringing painfully in their ears. Its brittle, shrill note seemed to stab their eardrums like a knife.

Looking to the windows of the stronghouse, another thirty strides ahead of them, they were shocked to see every pane of glass was lit up with flames! The flames danced, flickered and dazzled. Had the McCarthys set the place on fire? No, surely not! The two men struggled to make sense of what they were seeing and looked around them in consternation.

It was as if they had entered a dream. Alex and Hamish found themselves unable to control their pace. Their headlong dash had now turned into a slow, tortuous dawdle that felt like they were pushing their way upstream through an invisible river. Try as they might to maintain their speed, each stride seemed to take several seconds to complete.

Alex managed to turn his head, though with infuriating sluggishness, and saw four men all dressed head to toe in black. The men were sprinting towards them from a thicket of bushes. The man in the lead was shouting something, urgently, at them, but his voice had become such a preposterously slow drawl that they could not understand it.

At the same moment, Alex and Hamish reached the same conclusion. They might well be about to die.

CHAPTER 06

The Laird Grant heard the melancholy cry of the warning horn and stiffened. His face hardened, losing its (recently) amicable expression. In that fraction of a second, both Balgair and Gavin were satisfied that there was neither guile nor deception about this man. He was, they were both certain, as surprised and as worried as anybody else!

The Grant looked to his Senior Officers to gauge their reaction. Balgair and Gavin looked to them, too, to see if there would be a confrontation. The Grants appeared to have all been taken unawares.

As the note of the horn faded, there was a tinny whistling sound as the alarm arrow from the queen's encampment descended out of the sky. With its stream of ribbons rippling and flailing, it embedded itself into the grass, slightly upstream of them.

"Bobbins!" Shouted Gavin, "Go to back to the camp and bring back news. Run like the wind!"

Without hesitation, young Bobbins raced away like a hare fleeing a fox.

Annis said nothing. She simply backed her horse up and began to walk it down the riverbank. Her pace was slow and calculated, with no hint of haste.

Balgair and Gavin stood passively beside their horses.

"You two have not moved," The Grant observed.

"No, but we'll move soon enough," replied Balgair.

"You must have planned for every possible outcome of today, to remain so calm," The Grant responded, mildly amused.

"I have lived for far too many years on land bordering the Campbells not to consider the worst possible consequence for just about anything you can imagine!" Balgair snorted.

Both men laughed, naturally and unforced, and those nearby joined in. Just then, a Grant messenger arrived, breathless from his sprint, and spoke a few hurried words to the laird's Second-in-Command, Sandy McDowell. The message was then duly relayed to The Grant himself who, like a gambler picking up a new card from the table, showed no visible emotion. A few seconds elapsed before he spoke. When he did, it was curt and precise.

"We fight," said the laird.

The laird's officers, in response, stood tall and saluted.

"Your Lairdship!" Balgair protested, his manner indignant, "We of Clan MacDonald have your back!"

"I thank you," The Grant replied, his tone sincere, "We also have yours."

Sandy McDowell came forward and looked meaningfully from his leader to Gavin and Balgair, then back again. The laird held the other's gaze, coolly, for a few moments and then nodded.

"We have," began McDowell, "A strange circumstance befalling us."

Balgair exchanged a glance with Gavin, seeking inspiration, but Gavin's look was unmistakable: He had none to share.

"We seem to have been joined, to the North, by Clan Rose." McDowell announced, then added with copious contempt, "Our loyal allies."

This statement was greeted by muttered swearing from the Grant seniors and open hoots of derision from those further back. There was an ironic smile from The Grant, himself.

"They appear to bear the Clan MacDonald ill will," McDowell confided, with a grin.

This time, several of the Grant Seniors laughed out loud and one slapped his thigh in amusement. The smile from The Grant was now broad and unguarded.

"It would be a bold man who would be willing to gamble on whether they hate you or us the most!" McDowell declared, now unable to suppress his own laughter.

At that moment, there was a clinking of metal and a jingle of a harness, a short distance along the bank. Queen Annis appeared, astride her horse, heading towards them. She was clad, once more, in her armour and carried not her ceremonial sword but her heavy battle sword.

There was a slight commotion among the Grant escort and several of the seniors, too. Though nobody had spoken aloud, Balgair and Gavin both realised – in an instant – that they had taken the queen's subtle disappearance to have been her slipping away to safety.

The Laird Grant turned to his group and the look of pure contempt he gave them very nearly made the air crackle and spark. The culprits looked down at their feet, having the good manners to be ashamed.

The Grant watched Queen Annis approach and the look of pride in his eyes took Balgair by surprise. Balgair looked to Gavin who gave him a little smile. He, too, had seen the look. It was obvious that they were of a mind. They had both been inclined to like the Laird Grant, but now they also held him in the highest regard.

Annis had donned her bleached white tunic, again. It had been repaired with a carelessness that was diligent and precise, for it left the bright metal of her armour beneath it conspicuously visible at several strategic points.

"Your Highness," Gavin said, bowing, "The Laird Grant has been joined by a force, to the North, whose allegiance and intentions appear hostile."

"Given the choice of either slitting the throats of Grants or MacDonalds," Balgair announced, "They are left scratching their heads trying to decide!"

"They appear to have arrived as our allies," the Laird Grant disclosed, "But their loyalty is as unpredictable as the direction of the wind."

"Allies?" Annis queried, tilting her head.

"Allies against your army," The Grant replied, apologetically, "But there is little love lost between they and us, so I doubt that they would find it hard to turn their hand to mischief!"

There was a loud splashing from the river and they all turned to see Bobbins making his way across, leaping and jumping to gain more speed. He reached the sand and grit of the shoreline and came stumbling - shivering and spluttering as he went – up the rise to firm ground.

At first, he headed towards Gavin, before spotting the queen on her horse, and promptly veered off towards her, in preference. As he drew near, he threw himself to the ground and prostrated himself.

"Stand! Stand!" Annis urged him, leaping from her saddle to land nimbly beside him.

The boy declined to get to his feet, but knelt up tall, instead. Trembling from either cold or fear, he cupped his hands in front of his mouth like a funnel. The queen leaned forward and put her ear close, to receive the message. As she listened her face displayed a sequence of different emotions, progressing from worry, to disappointment, to alarm and finally reaching grim resignation.

Annis climbed back into her saddle, deploying an acrobatic grace that defied the weight of her armour, and eased her horse across to Balgair and Gavin.

"We have word from our rear guard." Annis declared, gesturing over her shoulder to the far side of the Spey, "There is a force fast approaching our encampment. It is bent on attack."

Her audience looked to her with eager anticipation, but they did not climb back into their saddles.

"The Campbells and their followers," Annis told them, "Don't seem able to wait to simply pick off the survivors of any battle with the Grants and have come to do the job themselves."

"The Campbells are no friends of ours!" The Grant exclaimed.

There was a chorus of dark mutterings and thinly disguised curses from the assembled Grants.

"These MacDonalds have only brought a token force with them!" The Grant's heir protested, indignantly.

"Is this true?" The laird asked, looking at Balgair in mock astonishment.

"I'm sure I don't know what you are talking about!" Replied Balgair shrugging his shoulders and pulling his face into an imitation of wounded pride.

The Grant held Balgair with a steady gaze.

"I am but a sheep," Captain Balgair protested, "Wandering, timidly, among a pack of wolves!"

The Grant smiled and arched an eyebrow. Balgair looked to their queen and saluted her, before turning back to the Laird Grant.

"I have at least another five hundred fellow sheep who have, purely by chance, wandered in this same direction," Balgair confessed, lifting both palms to the sky to declare his innocence, "A mere co-incidence, though a welcome one."

"So many for my brave few?" Asked Annis, accusingly.

Balgair looked so affronted that she immediately regretted her sarcasm.

"Your Majesty," announced Balgair, "We only became aware of reinforcements being on their way when a message arrived just as we were about to cross the river."

The queen's expression softened.

"We came here to protect you," Balgair asserted, "But to do so without drawing aggression down on you by sporting too large a force. It would appear that, since our departure, things have moved on and our limited numbers have acted as an irresistible lure to the Campbells."

"The MacDonald appears to have covered every option!" Gavin proclaimed.

Annis raised her hand to quell any further exchanges.

"I know," Annis admitted, "That any McRory would be stranded if things were to go badly this far East. I am wise enough to realise that you were sent for that exact reason."

Balgair looked glum, for he had come to the same conclusion.

"In the sight of the gods," Annis announced, "We are – all of us – no more than mice or maggots."

She waved her hand in the air, dismissively, and shrugged her shoulders, making her steel breastplate rise and fall.

"Monarchs, dukes, knights and peasants," she told them, "Are all the same when they are rotting in the ground!"

She raised her voice to reach the greater assembly of soldiers, unsheathing her sword and holding it aloft for them to see.

"Those who command power usually regard a soldier's life as worthless," she told them.

There was a general murmuring and muttering of approval among those gathered. The sound was most prominent and sustained amongst the lower ranks.

"I am Annis. I am Queen of the West. I am here and I stand beside you."

This was greeted by a loud chorus of cheering and bellowing of encouragement that rippled, as quick as a flash, up to and across the common soldiers.

"I give you this pledge," Annis cried, at the top of her voice, "That if this day should cost any man his life, I will have flowers placed on their grave and I will recite their name and bless them, at sunset and at sunrise for the next seven days."

Annis leaned towards the Laird Grant, Balgair and Gavin and shouted to them as the din of the troops began to rise.

"Let our common enemy, up on the hill, hear us and know us to be united! If they were unsure of us, let us make them certain!"

The roar of the troops lifted rapidly into a thundering wall of noise. Even the mighty uproar and clamour of earlier in the day was totally surpassed. The yelling, howling and chanting boomed in all directions. This was quickly joined by the blasting and blaring of horns and the siren wail of bagpipes.

The ear-splitting torrent of their vocal enthusiasm throbbed and thrummed in the air like a physical fog of noise and could be heard to roll back and forth from one flank of the army to the other as if each wing were Hell bent on outdoing the other!

After three continuous minutes, the performance showed no signs of abating, and the Grant seniors looked, from one to the other, in disbelief and amazement.

Suddenly, the cacophony fell away, dropping to a dreadful silence in the space of a few seconds. A new sound could now be heard in the distance. It came from beyond the meadows. It came from up the incline to the brow of the hill. It was the sound of the Clan Rose army. They were pouring down the slope towards them, issuing a full-throated war cry as they came. They were a human wave of wrath and rage, in full charge.

"So," said Balgair conversationally, "To horse, then?"

The Laird Grant smiled sardonically as he replied.

"It seems like a nice day for a ride."

Annis laughed aloud at the absurdity of their manly capers. This, she knew, was very much like when the young boys, in her childhood, would stand on a bridge and see who could piss the furthest upstream. Balgair and The Grant may not be pissing, she decided, but their behaviour served the same competitive purpose.

The other horses were brought forward, having been readied but neglected for the last fifteen minutes, and everybody mounted up. When all straps were tightened and double checked by the attendants, they all moved forward to the edge of the field where the sand from the river petered out.

Annis motioned to Balgair and he called a solder across to him. Annis beckoned him and he came to stand beside her.

"Take my maid, my squire and the two girls and hasten them to safety," she commanded, "Mark my words when I say this: Guard them with your life."

"Take five other men with you, to ensure it," barked Balgair.

"My Queen!" Morag cried, "I will fight! I can wield both bow and sword. You know this!"

"No!" Annis exclaimed, "I cannot spare you. Take the children and go. Keep them safe!"

Morag reluctantly obeyed and trudged off to join the soldiers who were hurrying Bobbins, Jet and Jade away into the trees and back towards the hills.

Annis spurred Bliss away and they all trotted up towards the gathering conflict. As Balgair had expected, the Laird Grant's men had already wheeled about and were now facing the charging foe. The pike men had gone forward and now had their long, elegant weapons laid touching the soil in readiness to be hoisted.

"An English weapon best used against horses," remarked The Grant, seeing what had caught Balgair's attention, "But they can fell twenty or more soldiers on foot, at six or seven paces, before they are close enough to use their steel."

Balgair, and Gavin by his side, nodded approvingly.

"A dead man is a dead man, however he falls," Gavin declared, philosophically.

The laird nodded in reply and then made a fair pretence at a leisurely stretch.

"A two minute charge on foot," The Grant announced, "From the top of the ridge to my front line. At my calculations, less than a minute has elapsed."

Nobody said anything in reply and the laird smiled to himself, enjoying the game. Balgair smiled back, knowing that he had an ace up his sleeve.

"Advance!" Shouted Balgair, abruptly, projecting his voice to his left.

In a moment, thirty MacDonald and Brydda troops emerged from the cover of the trees, upstream.

The Grant threw a sharp look of reproach at McDowell.

"My Laird, I knew they were there!" McDowell protested, "By the time they arrived in the trees, the whole of us were already sworn allies!"

The Grant looked only slightly placated and watched the troops come forward. He appeared more than a little interested in the twenty English longbows carried by the McRorys amongst their number.

"An English weapon," Gavin quipped, "Best used against anybody foolish enough to get in their way!"

They all laughed, including Annis, who had seen the destructive force of a longbow, at close range. It had been when she was a child and that day was cruelly etched into her memory.

Their opponents, five hundred strong, were now only a short distance away. Gavin thrust his finger into the air, as if pointing to the sun, and there was an immediate swooshing sound as sixty arrows, each notched in pairs, leapt skyward. The graceful arc of death drew itself high across the field like an angry swarm of wasps and came to earth amongst the second and third ranks of the attackers.

"Your archers are impressive," the Laird Grant commended, "They have shot a huge distance."

"Thank you," replied Balgair, "They have the shoulders of oxen!"

Next, they heard thunder. A pounding, rolling thunder. It was not from the sky above them. It was not echoing from the valley walls beyond. A few who did not understand looked around in confusion. Those who knew, smiled a dark smile and pursed their lips in approval.

Suddenly, forty horsemen of the McRory cavalry burst out from the nearby trees, their light armour flashing and gleaming in the bright sunshine. The riders had started their charge by riding, at full tilt, down the grass bank behind the foliage and had built up a tremendous momentum. This, they used to dramatic effect as they ploughed into the side of their quarry.

Soldiers of the Clan Rose were physically lifted into the air and thrown head over heels as the rampaging horses smashed into them. Even five strides beyond the original point of impact, men were still being thrown to either side like rag dolls, their bodies broken and mangled even before they hit the ground.

"Will you send me men to teach my soldiers to fight on horseback?" Asked The Grant.

"Yes. I will. I swear it," Balgair assured him.

The Laird Grant watched in rapt amazement as the horses, themselves, became a weapon in their own right. The protective curved metal plates they wore – to guard their chests, upper legs, knees and shins – struck the opposing fighters like a flurry of blacksmiths hammers, shattering ribs and splintering arm and thigh bones like twigs.

Now buried deep into the oncoming army, the cavalry horses came to a halt. The riders of this attacking formation promptly slumped forward against the necks of their steeds to brace themselves in readiness. Without a command, and as naturally as if they were drinking or eating, the outer wall of these furious beasts spun to the side and, leaning onto their front legs, kicked their back legs into the swirl of human bodies to their rear. They repeated this action, over and over again, shattering skulls, caving in chests and breaking spines. The horses slowly and methodically turned in an arc as they fought, carefully distributing their blistering fury to all within their reach. The attackers fell back in widening circles around the kicking horses. Their riders responded by quickly spurring their mounts forward, pushing into the throng in all directions. Gripping their strangely contoured saddles with their thighs to remain seated, the riders unsheathed twin swords and, holding one in each hand, proceeded to slash and cut down at their foes to devastating effect.

"I am impressed!" Called the Laird Grant over the noise.

As the outer group of riders dispersed, the inner part of the mounted column moved forward, pushing deeper into the fray like a ram. Suddenly, their horses, too, came to a halt and – repeating the earlier actions of their fellows – began to spin around, kicking out their back legs, and reversing up into the crowd until nobody was left close enough to hit. Again, when they had run out of victims, they were powered forward, heading to all points of the compass, their riders wielding their twin blades with deadly efficiency.

The pikemen, from the Grant vanguard – more used to standing still – began to slowly walk forward, impaling the flagging soldiers ahead of them. The cavalry had caused such grand mayhem that their adversaries had failed to muster themselves and had not managed to breach this nightmare wall of ghastly porcupine quills. The pikes were driven into and through the advancing force to such effect that the men wielding them had difficulty freeing their weapons from their victims. Presently, the pikes – having skewered too many trophies to be manageable – were dropped to the ground and discarded.

As the pikes went down, the Grant force flooded forward into the Clan Rose, claymores and axes swishing and singing in the air. The attackers were now in disarray and finding it a challenge to maintain their ground. The Grants ran into their midst and hacked mercilessly at the shocked and reeling on-comers. Before long, they had worked their way through to the rear of the original force.

The bagpipes of the Grant army sounded and, in response, their troops fell back, compelling their opponents to come forward and climb over and through a carpet of their dead and dying clansmen to reach them. This appeared to have the demoralising effect that was intended and their vigour and determination began to wane.

At the far edge of the battle, the McRory horsemen, having cut their way through the melee to exit the far side of the combatants, wheeled around to the rear and came back into them.

After sending another two volleys into the far edge of the conflict, the MacDonald archers found there were no longer any distinct and isolated targets remaining. The command was given for them to join the fray, hand to hand.

Eventually, the forward rank of the Grants began to thin out – this being the inevitable result of fatalities – and a breach began to form before their second rank could move forward to fill it. The Grant pipes quickly sounded an alarm.

Balgair and the Laird Grant exchanged a look. Neither needed the other's expression to be explained to them. Words, at that moment, had become completely redundant. They both knew that they might be staring at defeat.

CHAPTER 07

Right from her arrival at Brech Woorlach, Janine had been slightly puzzled by the reception she had received. Everything that had happened since had only increased that feeling.

She now found herself walking along the plush corridor from her chambers with the Duchess of Bo'Ness beside her and trailed by the twins and Francesca.

As they descended the beautiful marble stairs, decorated either side with exquisitely carved wooden panels, she fought to keep her mind from reeling. She was starting to have ever more intrusive memories of this place. Memories that, surely, could not be real.

She felt butterflies in her stomach as they crossed the marble-tiled floor of the palatial entrance and found the duke waiting for them. He inclined his head to her and touched his brow in a salute. Janine smiled and performed a curtsy and was dismayed to see that her display of respect caused him to appear uneasy.

Their party began down another set of stairs, lined with wooden panels that were yet more exquisite, still.

The route they were taking, Janine instinctively knew, led to the lower chambers set beneath Brech Woorlach. Brian and Bruce – sensing her to be ill at ease – smiled at her, reassuringly, when they caught her eye. She tried to smile back at them confidently, but she knew it to be a poor and unconvincing attempt.

At the bottom of the stairs, they entered a long corridor that led away into the distance underneath the building. One wall was punctuated, for its entire length, by narrow slots of windows that were arranged to channel the daylight from above ground.

Janine could not suppress an impossible recollection that the sumptuous and stylish decoration above ground level was neither subdued nor compromised below ground level. There, just as she knew they would be, were the rich fabrics, golden tassels, fine woodwork, bronze statues and shining brass fixtures. There, too, were the tapestries hung from the walls, the tasteful pictures in grand gold frames and bowls and vases stood on exquisitely fashioned pedestals.

As they approached an onyx table with ornate spiral legs, she could not resist the urge to pause and admire it. Much to her amazement, the duke and duchess stopped and waited, patiently, for her. Francesca and the twins did the same. She was disturbed and slightly alarmed by their air of deference, which she found increasingly unsettling.

Without intending to do it, and before she could prevent the action, she reached out to touch the gleaming polished surface of the table. The moment her fingers made contact, she hastily withdrew her hand and looked a little embarrassed.

"Please!" The duke urged and waved an elegantly manicured hand towards the table.

Janine cautiously placed her hand back onto the gleaming cold surface. She stroked it and drew her fingertips across it in little circles. The duchess stood by, waiting passively in the background, assuming the stance and disposition of some kind of attendant. Janine, captivated by the striking beauty of the onyx, ran her fingertips across its surface, again.

"It is completely and utterly beautiful!" Janine declared.

"If the table meets your approval," the duchess told her, "Then I can arrange for it to be installed in your chambers. It would be no trouble at all."

Unable to make her mind work properly, Janine mumbled a reply, in a state of distraction.

"It is very kind of you to offer," she said.

Janine realised that she had inadvertently delayed their progress longer than she had been aware and looked to the duke to apologise. To her complete bafflement the duke faltered and then gave her an obliging smile. Janine's heart stopped and lurched for a moment in her chest. She knew that smile! She had given it to her betters a hundred times before, as a maid. Seeing it on the face of the duke left her completely bewildered.

Janine took a step along the corridor and her escort politely moved off behind her, the five of them meekly picking up her pace. Janine suddenly wondered if she were in a dream. She pondered whether she might be about to wake up and feel woefully embarrassed for having such a weird and idiotic fantasy! This, after all, could not possibly be really happening. In no realm of real life, she knew, anywhere on this Earth, did a duke and duchess bow their heads to a domestic servant!

Janine began to notice a vague aroma in the air and inhaled it deeply. She now recognised it as incense. It was a very pleasant smell, she decided. It was not the kind of incense used in church, which was usually bitter and acrid, but something wonderfully fragrant and mellow. She suddenly snatched at her train of thought. That was nonsense! She had never been to a church that could have ever afforded such a luxury as incense. In which case, how could she possibly know? She groaned, inwardly, and tucked away this little observation as another example of her bizarre and troublesome situation.

Towards the far end of the luxuriously carpeted hallway, the lamps on the walls gave way to Chinese lanterns. These were burning scented oil and, combined with the incense, they made a heady concoction. The statues and ornaments that lined the walls had now become dragons and tigers. Set into the very end wall were a pair of richly lacquered, glossy red doors decorated with Chinese symbols written in gold. Above the elaborate brass handles, split left and right across the gap between the two doors, was a Chinese word-graphic embellished with swirling flourishes.

"Destiny," said Janine, touching the word with her finger.

How could she possibly know that? Again, she felt the now familiar pang of recollection and confusion mixed into one and cringed at the pain it caused in her head.

Out of the corner of her eye, Janine detected a subtle glance from the duke and duchess and felt the twins' gaze fall on her for a brief moment. Francesca had looked purposefully away, making a pretence of being distracted.

The duchess took hold of a little brass chain that was set to one side of the doors. She gently pulled the chain to the full extent of its travel. From the other side of the doors, within the chamber beyond them, there was the dull, echoing sound of a gong.

After a few moments, the door was opened by a young, slim and very pretty Chinese girl who was wearing what Janine, inexplicably, knew to be a traditional Chinese dress. She bowed low to each of them in turn, her eyes firmly on the carpet, and then ushered them inside.

As they passed the girl, she looked up and, on seeing Janine, her face lit up with a huge smile. Janine shot a desperate look at Francesca but found her to be diligently examining her fingernails. There was no doubt that this girl was radiantly happy to see her. For a fleeting moment, Janine looked puzzled, before gathering herself and swiftly smiling back.

They entered a long room with a log fire at its far end. The fireplace was tall and wide, but the black, wrought iron trough that sat below its arched roof had but a single large log burning at its centre and seemed dwarfed by the surrounding stonework.

The walls of the chamber were made of bare stone, but finely carved with a series of intricate columns and ledges. There were lots of little alcoves, at regular intervals down either wall, and each of them held a small oil lamp that was lit with a glowing dull orange flame. The effect was amazing. It was, Janine thought, like the walls were floating in the air.

There was a small table in front of the fire with a high-backed chair drawn up to it. In the chair sat a small, thin Chinese man with a kind face and extremely intelligent eyes. He smiled at Janine and his smile made her feel deeply peaceful and at ease. This, she realised, must be Mister Chang. No! That was ridiculous! How could she possibly know his name?

The man stood as they approached and bowed to each of them in turn, just as the girl had done. Each member of the duke and duchess' party bowed back and Janine followed their example. The man gestured to chairs set in a semi-circle a little way back from the table and they all sat down. The duke declined the middle chair, positioned opposite the Chinese gentleman, and the duchess motioned for Janine to sit there.

There was a silence. Since nobody else spoke, Janine held the silence. It was a comfortable silence. They were, she discerned, waiting for something. After a minute the young Chinese girl came in, emerging from an entrance in the wall hidden by a curtain. She was carrying a tray laden with the paraphernalia for making tea.

The girl arranged the tea things carefully on the table. After selecting a whisk and several other utensils, she busied herself with the preparing of the tea, studiously and meticulously following a sequence of time-honoured steps. Everybody watched her, entranced by her care and diligence, as her hands moved gently and gracefully about the task.

Once the ritual was complete, everybody drew their chairs to the table and the girl handed out a small stone bowl to each person. She poured tea into every bowl and then quietly made her exit. The assembled individuals waited for Janine to sip her tea, first, then they waited for Mister Chang to sip his before venturing to drink, themselves. Janine found this slightly unsettling.

There were only a few, brief words spoken while they drank their tea. These were limited to formal pleasantries, here and there, but nothing of any substance was addressed. Janine understood that this was a preamble to conversation and that the polite behaviour being observed required nothing of significance to be attempted at this point.

Ten minutes passed until all their bowls were drained and placed back on the table. As if by magic, the girl appeared – seemingly from nowhere – and cleared everything away quickly and efficiently. She moved with lithe agility. The fluidity of her motions had a captivating elegance about them.

The young Chinese girl's name suddenly came into Janine's head. It was Genji! This she knew – for no reason she could possibly fathom – that this meant "òr" in Gaelic or "gold" in English.

Mister Chang respectfully lowered his head to Janine, to the duke and to the duchess.

"I have received and read your note with great interest," he told the duke, "I can feel the irresistible pull of fate at work in recent events."

The duke nodded, wisely.

"The cogs and wheels of life," Mister Chang continued, "Sometimes turn slowly and sometimes turn quickly. Whatever their speed, their effect is unstoppable and relentless."

Mister Chang paused and looked at Janine for a moment. In that instant it dawned on Janine that whilst he was speaking to the duke, his message was actually aimed at her.

"Different cultures and religions around the world have long attempted to explain how and why events occur at exactly at the right time and in the right order, to bring about a particular outcome. What we call this force, or how we account for it, is of far less importance than that we simply accept it for what it is."

The room had fallen into rapt silence.

"There are times, however, when – like a leaf rushing down a river, that constantly finds the fastest route over and around obstacles – one set of events that seem to dash on ahead, leaving others to hang and tarry at a slower pace."

None of his listeners moved or said a word.

"Things that appear to happen out of order, in the course of history, are every bit as important as those events that appear to progress in harmony. It is not required that we understand life and its grand purpose. We have no more need to know its meaning than a seed that is blown in the wind or a drop of rain that falls from the clouds."

Mister Chang stood up and moved behind his chair.

"I could move this chair to one side of this table or to the other. The chair doesn't need to be told why and it cannot raise a voice to ask. A piece of furniture has no mind, no thought and no understanding. It can neither give nor withhold its consent."

Mister Chang sat back down.

"Human beings, on the other hand, are an entirely different matter. Some say that we, as people, are simply pieces in a board game. This may or may not be true, but it is certain that a playing piece never seeks to help or hinder the outcome of the game. People like to think that they can sway their fate, this way or that, but it is an illusion. Whatever they do or fail to do is exactly what was needed and exactly what was intended."

They all listened, attentively, completely enthralled by Mister Chang's words.

"Life is brutal and can inflict pain and misery that is neither necessary nor even justifiable and, sometimes, it can even be counterproductive. If you put your finger into the gears of a milling machine, it will keep on turning, regardless, and will reduce your finger to a bloody mess."

Mister Chang's audience all winced at this comparison and Janine flicked her eyes around the other's faces to register their responses. As a result, it was a moment or two before Janine realised that Mister Chang was now looking solely at her.

"I need to take your finger out of the machine," he told her, "For what is happening to you, lately, is causing you suffering and confusion and it risks causing injury to your mind."

Janine felt all eyes on her. She was conscious that her lip had begun to tremble. She could feel herself on the verge of tears. She realised that some stupid and absurd misunderstanding had occurred over the last few days, and that these good people had completely confused her identity. She had been mistaken for being somebody else and, by putting off confronting them about it, she had only succeeded in making things worse. She was overwhelmed by their kindness and the idea of having to, finally, confess to them and cause them disappointment filled her with unbearable grief.

"You have confused me with somebody else," Janine began, a tear rolling down her cheek, "For somebody that I am not."

The duchess' face crumpled and her eyes welled with tears. She leaned forward and reached out to touch Janine's arm, but then drew back at the last moment, her hand now hanging uncertainly in the air.

"Touch me!" Janine implored, dragging the hand of the duchess down to rest on her own, "Why would you think you may not?"

The duchess now began to cry, unrestrained, and brought her other hand to rest on Janine's.

"Oh! My Lady!" The duchess gasped, her voice breaking with emotion.

"Me? Your lady?" Janine yelped in sudden outrage, "You are my lady! For you are a duchess and I am nothing more than a silly runaway servant girl! I am so very sorry that Brian and Bruce, of your house, have falsely – yet with good intention – portrayed me as anything else to you."

Janine was now weeping, herself, and her chest was heaving with the weight of her sorrow. She had finally reached breaking point. She felt utterly ashamed of herself for having left it so late to shatter their illusions and expose herself as an imposter.

"I am a nobody!" Janine protested, her voice several octaves higher than she had intended, "I am a no-one!"

Janine was startled to see the duchess pull her hands away and clasp them, one over the other, in a combined fist in front of her mouth and begin shaking with inconsolable anguish. The twins reached out, each putting a hand on one of her shoulders, and both looked distraught.

"Your Ladyship…," Francesca began, in a tremulous voice.

Janine whirled on her friend, now furious, and howled at her indignantly.

"Don't call me that!"

Francesca recoiled in horror, as if she had been slapped, and then she, too, began to cry.

"Why do you call me that?" Janine implored, her voice now softened to a more conciliatory tone.

"Because," Brian announced in exasperation, "She fears using the proper form of address to you because it risks causing you even greater confusion and alarm!"

Janine's face fell into an expression of total disbelief and she stared at the little group incredulously.

"Please!" The duchess begged, turning to Mister Chang, and sobbing as if in mortal torment, "No more! No more! No more!"

Mister Chang looked back at her passively, at first, but then his air of detachment slowly melted and his face took on, instead, a look of deep sadness.

"Very well," he replied, with evident reluctance and nodded solemnly.

"What would you call me, then?" Janine asked him, leaping to her feet in annoyance.

At this point, as if a secret signal had been given. The five of them – the duke, the duchess, Brian, Bruce and Francesca – all dropped to their knees in a line. Janine stared at them, unable to make sense of what was happening.

"I would call you Your Majesty!" He replied.

CHAPTER 08

Janine could not believe her ears. What possible reason could anybody have to refer to her as 'Your Majesty'? She was as far from being a majesty as a tabby cat was from being a lion!

She surveyed the scene before her, but her mind could not properly grasp or comprehend it. She looked at each of the people in turn. The Duke of Bo'Ness, his wife, The Duchess of Bo'Ness, their adopted sons, Brian and Bruce and their daughter, Francesca. All of them were on their knees with their heads bowed. This even included Mister Chang, the Chinese expert in ancient healing and of fighting arts. She had presumed that he would have been above such things.

"What did you say?" Janine gasped in astonishment, "What did you call me?"

She took a step back, accidentally colliding with her chair.

"I called you, Your Majesty," Francesca repeated, "For that is your title."

Janine looked across the table at Mister Chang and made a forlorn gesture of enquiry to him, the sweep of her hand taking in everyone on their knees.

"In all parts of the world," Mister Chang replied, "It is a tradition that the subjects of a monarch kneel to show respect."

"Mister Chang," said Janine, earnestly, "I am no monarch. I am a mere servant. I am the personal maid of the Lady Dunkeld, or I was, until...."

Her voice trailed off as she considered how much she should reveal of recent events. It took only a second for her to decide that the more detail she disclosed, the surer they would be of their mistake.

"I left that role, when... No, I did not leave, I ran away. I ran away when the Sergeant-at-Arms there began paying me intrusive and shameful attention."

The people knelt before her listened intently.

"I told her ladyship what was happening, but she did not believe me. Things got worse and worse. He became more and more forceful. One day he tried to force himself on me. He would have raped me but for a rescuer who intervened. He killed my attacker. I fainted and woke up alone. I found the Sergeant-at-Arms in a pool of blood. His corpse had been severely battered."

Mister Chang turned his head, very slightly, to give the Duke of Bo'Ness, who was knelt beside him, a knowing look from the corner of his eye.

'What is it that he knows?' Janine wondered.

"I panicked. I ran away. I made my escape from Dunkeld Manor with a young boy. His name is Callum. He and I arrived here together. Callum was being ill-treated and he, too, was desperate to get away. We had not travelled far when we were confronted by a group of bandits. I sent the boy to hide and managed to run from them. I thought I had escaped, but one of them caught me. He was about to set about me when I was rescued, again. I don't remember anything about that, except that I found myself waking up on the ground, unharmed. On searching around me, I discovered that the bandit had been brutally slain and his body dragged into some nearby greenery."

Mister Chang nodded, seeming unsurprised by her extraordinary tale.

"The boy and I somehow managed to find our way back to the road and, by a stroke of luck, we were picked up and brought here to Brech Woorlach by the wonderful twin brothers Brian and Bruce."

Janine recalled, vividly, how — from the very first moment that she laid her eyes on Brech Woorlach — she had been perturbed by its familiarity.

"Brian and Bruce," The Duke of Bo'Ness declared, "Did not know, at the time, that they had encountered a queen."

"A queen?" Janine exclaimed, "You are mistaken! That is simply not so!"

"It is most definitely so, Your Majesty," The Duke insisted, "For you are, without a shadow of a doubt, the rightful and true born Queen of the West!"

Janine blinked at him, aghast. She knew of the Queen of the West, but only as some lofty and distant inspiration. She had no concept of her as a person of flesh and blood. She was not anybody she would ever hope to meet, not even in a dozen lifetimes! Surely, she reasoned, members of royalty were from a whole different world and not one that she would ever encounter.

Janine shook her head in disbelief, "You are mistaken!" She insisted.

"There is no mistake!" The Duke assured her.

"None whatsoever!" The Duchess agreed.

"You are Queen Cydara's daughter," the Duke declared, "You are the rightful Queen of the West."

"But..." Janine protested, her mind spinning, "We all know of Queen Annis, the warrior queen in the Highlands. If it is I who am the Queen of the West, then who is she?"

"An imposter," the Duchess said firmly, "A decoy, perhaps, set up by your mother's enemies to confuse those who would search for you."

"Or possibly a Campbell puppet," the Duke suggested, "Claiming a title that is yours by blood."

"Your mother told us that you were her only child," said the Duchess, "Everything we have done has been to protect you until it was safe for you to claim your throne."

When Janine looked to Francesca, however, she saw something flicker in her eyes. A doubt, perhaps, or maybe a secret very carefully kept?

From the corner of her eyes, Janine caught the Duke making a thinly disguised gesture to Mister Chang.

"Your Majesty," said Mister Chang, standing and bowing deeply, "It is you who mistakes your identity, not us. I regret to inform you that – in this respect – I am the one who is mostly to blame."

Janine looked at the Chinese man with undisguised suspicion.

"Your arrival here, Your Majesty," Mister Chang informed her, "Is by a cruel twist of fate that has inflicted unbearable torment on your mind. For it was never intended that you should ever see this place, again, in your lifetime."

Janine's look of distrust only increased.

"It is best," The Duke assured her, "If Mister Chang tells you everything, so that we can stop this ghastly charade as quickly as we can."

Mister Chang's daughter, Genji, suddenly wafted into view. Quickly and gracefully, she drew a set of comfortable chairs to form a crescent in front of the fire. They all sat down. Genji built up the fire with more logs before dropping to sit, cross-legged, to one side of the hearth.

"For your own protection and safety," Mister Chang began, "You have grown up wholly unaware of your real identity. When you were small, there were those who plotted against you and who wished to do you harm."

Mister Chang's audience all nodded their agreement.

"We could think of no better way to hide you from others," he declared, "Than to hide you from yourself."

CHAPTER 09

The innkeeper and former navy adventurer, Hamish Pottle, watched in complete fascination as all motion around him slowed to a snail's pace. He swallowed hard, for he knew that this strange transformation only happened to a person when they were in extreme danger. Having lived a hazardous life, with mortal peril an all too frequent companion, he had become more familiar with the phenomenon than he might have wished. The human brain's ability to accelerate thought and perception by up to twenty times, at such moments of crisis, both awed and exhilarated him.

Close by, Alex Brenan was similarly enthralled by this slowing of time. Having recently returned to Scotland from Austria, where he had been fighting as a soldier in The Long War, he had encountered it once before. Convinced that he would never experience it again, he was shamelessly revelling in the moment.

Alex, who had taken up rooms at the inn that Hamish ran with his wife, Caitlan, had not hesitated when Hamish had invited him on a reckless escapade. He and Hamish were mounting a brave attempt to free another lodger at the inn from detention and likely execution by the McCarthys, a gang of local thugs.

The other lodger in question, whom they were trying to rescue, was Ewan Burberry, a constable from Edinburgh. A huge bear of a man, Burberry, it transpired, was on important business of King James. Despite having an escort of around thirty soldiers at his disposal, led by the very able Captain McCleary, the Constable had slipped away from them and had been kidnapped while out riding on his own.

Hamish and Alex, as they heroically charged the fortified stronghouse of the Constable's kidnappers, were shocked to find a group of four men, dressed head to toe in black, rushing in their direction from either side.

Lowering their heads to apply themselves even more strenuously to their outrageously slow gallop, both Hamish and Alex found themselves unable to accelerate. The two men cursed the agonising dawdle of their running, but realised that – in what might be termed "real life" – they would actually have been making a good pace.

Ahead of them, Alex and Hamish saw another four men, identically clad in the same black, emerge from dense foliage to the left and right. They carried between them a heavy battering ram, capped by a bull's head cast in iron, suspended from short ropes. The heavy weight of the ram forced them to purposely lean outward under the strain and sway, rhythmically, from side to side as they ran.

Suddenly, the leaping and curling flames that had mysteriously illuminated the windows of the stronghouse, became dim and misty, rendering the panes of glass translucent. Two faces were revealed behind them, peering out from the gloom.

Alex and Hamish raised the muskets they carried and took aim.

Alex targeted the face on the left, inexplicably knowing that Hamish had targeted the one on the right. They were both certain that neither face was that of the man they were rescuing, Constable Burberry.

With agonising slowness, they squeezed their triggers. The mechanisms, normally almost instantaneous, seemed to operate at the same feeble speed as a monotonously dripping tap. As their weapons discharged, erupting in languid flame and billowing lazy smoke, they felt the kick as heavy lead musket balls sped towards their quarry.

Alex and Hamish heard a series of loud bangs to either side of them. Their brains processed the noises, with lightning speed, to identify them as pistol shots. Somebody had given an order for the other four men in black to fire. Relieved that they were not the target, Alex and Hamish watched as the shots that had been fired gently strolled through the air. With the absent-minded distraction of day dreamers, they counted the blurred trail of all the streaking spheres and reached a tally of six.

The eight lithe and athletic black clad figures in this sluggish choreography now began to "dash" in earnest.

Alex and Hamish – taking advantage of their blisteringly rapid thoughts – cast their eyes over them and began to identify tell-tale points that revealed them as members of the military. These included the pattern of stitching on their canvas footwear, the king's crown emblem on the trailing metal ends of their ribbon-thin belts and the royal thistle on the pins that gathered their hoods at either side of their necks.

The musket balls despatched by Alex and Hamish were slightly ahead of their rivals and the uncanny accuracy of them was becoming evident. They were heading perfectly centred at the foreheads of their targets. They were either truly wonderous shots, they reflected, or – if what they suspected were true – they were shots influenced by a powerful force that was not of this world.

The two men inside the McCarthy stronghouse, as they looked out, had only just begun to focus on the scene that greeted them. They were not yet aware of their fate. For them, in the realm of ordinary time, only a couple of seconds had elapsed. Even if they had been blessed with the most nimble of minds, they would have had no time to react.

Alex could not suppress a smile as the first vague glimmer of realisation began to form on the faces of the men.

It was just occurring to them that they were being charged. It was less obvious whether either of them had registered the puffs of smoke from their attackers' weapons.

Another fifteen seconds seemed to drift by for Alex and Hamish. This was only two or three seconds for those within the fortified house. The two men, visible through the windows, now began to pull away from the glass. They had finally comprehended what was happening. Neither had made it more than half a step back before what seemed to be two large splashes of water appeared on the window pane in front of them.

Alex and Hamish were able to analyse what they saw, using the copious thinking time at their disposal, and recognised that the apparent 'liquid' was actually tiny particles of glass erupting from the window as their musket shots struck and pierced them. It looked for all the world like a pebble had been dropped into a pond, causing a perfectly circular crown of water to form.

A moment later, a black hole appeared at the centre of each man's brow and their heads abruptly snapped back. It was as if somebody had just hauled violently on their hair from behind. At the back of either man's skull, a hole the size of an adult fist appeared, from which a grey sludge, that was their brains, began to fall out and descend to the floor.

Snapping back from the distraction, Alex and Hamish found their attention drawn to the men in black. The first four had thrown themselves flat against the wall of the building, either side of the window.

The men carrying the ram swung it forward and upward. The ram drifted idly through the air at a leisurely pace. Presently, it struck the upright wooden beam in the middle of the window frame. Alex and Hamish watched as the beam bowed inwards, causing every pane of glass to break. The glass shattered into thousands of tiny shards that flew into the air like a flock of startled sparrows.

The timber of the adjoining beams split and fractured, above and below the point of impact, buckling inwards. The wood didn't have to move far before it made contact with the metal bars behind. The ram shuddered as its bludgeoning momentum transferred to the bars, causing the soldiers wielding it to stagger. At either side of the windows, a dusty cloud of powdered mortar lazily erupted as the fixings that held the bars in place were wrenched out of the blockwork. This was followed by a shower of stone fragments that spun and buzzed through the air like angry insects.

Alex and Hamish skidded and lurched to a halt, throwing their muskets to the ground and holding their hands in front of them to protect themselves from the flying debris. Unable to stop in time, they collided with the backs of the men wielding the battering ram. All parties came to a halt in an awkward huddle.

"Up!" Shouted one of the soldiers.

Neither Alex nor Hamish were quite sure if he were speaking to them or urging on his comrades, but they both obligingly gripped a pair of muscular calves and hoisted their owners bodily aloft. The soldiers, thus propelled onto the window sill, scrabbled with their feet for purchase. Recovering their footing, they jumped into the building, only to find several burning orbs of oil-soaked hay whizzing past their heads. Coming dangerously close, the fiery objects landed on the stone flagged floor, inside, their billowing flames illuminating the interior with a shocking brilliance.

The three McCarthy men who remained alive in the room, shielded their eyes from the blinding light and fired their twin pistols wildly. Six shots rang out. The noise in the confined space was deafening. The soldiers they were trying to hit had already dropped flat to the ground and all narrowly missed being struck. Having come from the bright daylight outside, they were able to see quite well, despite the flames, and returned fire with superior accuracy.

Two of the three McCarthys were hit and reeled backwards under the force of the pistol rounds. One struck the wall so hard with their head that they lost consciousness before they died. The second, colliding with a shelf, battered their head heavily, and tottered two steps before dropping to their knees, disorientated. The third man was unscathed and dodged for cover.

Alex and Hamish, who had thrown themselves onto the window ledge, were peering into the room. Abruptly, time jumped back to normal, causing them both to gaze, uncertainly, at the proceedings for a couple of moments before regaining their senses.

"One is still alive," Alex hissed, aiming at a man on his knees who was rummaging on the floor for his weapon.

Alex fired his pistol. The sound of the shot crashed and boomed, rebounding off the walls like thunder. The ball caught its victim in his jaw, shattering it catastrophically, before exiting to leave a gaping wound in his neck. A moment later, one of the two soldiers discharged their reserve pistol, delivering a ball through the man's temple which split his head like a coconut struck by a hammer.

Another McCarthy appeared in a doorway and, dropping into a crouch, turned sideways to minimise himself as a target. It was to no avail. Hamish put a shot through the man's shoulder, spinning him around, as the shot from the other soldier's second pistol took him squarely in the chest.

First Alex, then Hamish, were pushed flat against the stone sill as another four soldiers clambered over them and threw themselves into the mayhem inside. The acrid stench of spent gunpowder was overwhelming and so was the smell of scorched flesh and burning furniture and fittings. The new arrivals covered their mouths while their colleagues, already there, covered their ears.

More soldiers arrived outside the window and Alex and Hamish were dragged, unceremoniously, aside as lit torches were passed in while the new entrants, using pitchforks, hurled out the three incandescent orbs of hay that had originally provided illumination.

There were no further shots fired and the shock and tension palpably decreased by a notch or two. Captain McCleary – who had newly arrived on the scene – announced that there was no sign of the constable.

Alex and Hamish looked at each other with increasing alarm. If the soldiers had not found the constable inside, had he already been taken away somewhere? Worse still, had other members of their gang executed him, when they had heard the assault begin?

They heard shouts from inside and the stomping of several pairs of boots, followed by the noise of doors being kicked down. There was a sudden shuffling and jostling on the stairs and a loud crack as a weapon was fired. Alex and Hamish tried to attract the attention of Captain McCleary, who was locked in an animated conversation with his Second-in-Commend, but he deliberately ignored them. They had been officially relegated to mere bystanders.

Hamish shrugged and walked a little distance back from the house. Alex saw him stoop to pick something up from the mud and, when he straightened, he was holding one of the hunting muskets. Alex looked around and noted, glumly, that everything that was happening was completely without their involvement. Hamish quickly retrieved the other musket and held it up to Alex. Alex took it and tilted his head in silent question. Hamish gave him a weary smile and, slinging his own musket over his shoulder, began trudging across the rutted mud to their previous hiding place.

Alex considered hurrying after his friend, but decided against it, not wanting to stand out and draw attention. Instead, mimicking the listless gait that Hamish had adopted, he slouched and dawdled after him.

CHAPTER 10

When they reached the trees, Hamish halted and turned towards the stronghouse. His face was contemplative and, after a pause, his features transformed into a cunning smirk.

"You're right," said Hamish.

"I am?"

"Yes," Hamish replied.

"What did I say?"

"You said that this was 'The Quickening'."

"That's how it feels," Alex confirmed, "The flames were the final piece of the puzzle. It feels just so…."

"So?"

"So much like…."

"Like what?"

"Like destiny," said Alex.

Hamish raised his eyebrows.

"It's almost like we've walked onto the stage in a theatre while a play is being performed," Alex explained, "And, whilst we haven't seen the script, we still know the plot and the actions, but more importantly, we know how it ends."

Hamish nodded in agreement.

"When I was a boy, Hamish, my mother used to say: *'Alex, we all have a purpose in life, and – before it's over – either you will find it or it will find you.'*"

"A wise woman."

"God bless her."

"This is our purpose," Hamish said, emphatically, "And it's why we were born and why we have survived. It is our fate."

Alex nodded, slowly, and pursed his lips in a thin smile of grim acknowledgement. Hamish returned a fair approximation of the same dour look, without intending it.

They each lifted their musket and began to prepare them. They worked quickly and methodically, drying the sparking drum, scratching it with a pin to roughen it and wiping down all of the firing mechanisms. Next, they slid out the tamping rod from under the barrel, pulled out the stopper from their powder bags and dropped in a generous charge of gunpowder. They followed the charge with a lead ball and, sliding the tamping rod down the barrel, rammed it firmly into place. Next, they forced down a bung of moss to keep everything in place. Carefully, they each poured powder into the ignition pan and slid the cover closed. Finally, they rotated the sparking drum and listened to the satisfying dull click as it engaged.

Alex was just about to lift his musket to check the sights when Hamish placed his hand on his arm to stop him.

"Watch," he invited.

So saying, Hamish pointed to the butt of his firearm, where he flicked a little catch. Immediately, a compartment fell open and when Hamish tilted the weapon to one side, a pair of tiny glass discs fell out into his hand. Hamish reached out and put one of the discs in the line of Alex' vision and held it there. Alex, understanding that this was an invitation, looked through the disc. Engraved into its surface were two lines, one vertical and one horizontal, that crossed in the middle. This, he quickly worked out, was an aiming device. Hamish produced the second lens and held that one up, too. Alex peered through it and saw that the image that was beyond it was enlarged more than twice its original size. Alex watched as Hamish snapped first one and then the other lens into notches on the top of his musket.

"I see," Alex replied, smiling.

Quickly, Alex opened the same compartment on his own musket, and extracted the same cargo. Fixing one of the discs into the nearest notch above the barrel of his musket, he began to position and re-position it until he found the best of the six notches at the opposite end to suit his eyes.

All of a sudden, the two men stiffened and became keenly alert. Something was happening! They looked, first at each other, then around them. They had become aware of an eerie quiet. It was far too still and far too hushed to be the product of any natural source. A feeling had descended on the forest that was like an aura of calm. It felt like they were sitting in the pews of a cathedral.

Alex wagged his head like a dog emerging from a river that was shaking off water. Hamish reached up to the side of his own head and tapped his ear, disbelievingly. The two men looked at each other, neither breaking the silence.

Gradually, very faintly at first, they began to hear a sound that brought goose bumps to their flesh and made the hairs on their arms and the backs of their necks stand up. In this, otherwise noiseless theatre, the gentle crackling of a fire rose in volume until it became starkly audible. They looked around casually. Neither of them needed to be told that there would be no fire to see and, of course, there wasn't.

They watched the soldiers milling around, completely oblivious to the mysterious serenity of the moment. Little by little, they slowed and stood, responding to some kind of ethereal atmosphere that was gradually enveloping everyone. Within half a minute, all twenty of the visible troops had come to a halt and were just standing, passively, as if deep in thought.

The sun was heading towards the horizon, but there were still a couple of hours of light left. The stronghouse, however, was set back into the forest amongst a line of very tall, dense trees that – at this time of day – gave the immediate surroundings the effect of dusk.

Alex and Hamish knew that now was the time to act, but they were unable to explain why. They lifted up their muskets, together, and aimed them at the upper floor of the stronghouse. The interior of the rooms was dark and it was difficult to make out anything inside.

Suddenly, as if by magic, a ghostly orange glow appeared to illuminate the back of one of the rooms. It was as if the moon had risen and were bouncing off a mirror inside, except that there was no moon and there was no mirror.

CHAPTER 11

In the upstairs room within the McCarthy stronghouse, Constable Burberry shifted his weight slightly onto his left leg, his right one having begun to ache from standing still so long. The man with the pistol to his head growled a deep note of unmistakable warning that he should refrain. Burberry could not resist the urge to very slightly flex his wrists to move the cruel, biting pressure of his ropes to a different spot. He was rewarded with a jab in his temple from the pistol barrel and his head was rocked to the side.

Burberry pondered what he might possibly say to his captor that could sway his resolution, but discounted this as a ridiculous idea, considering the gag that was bound tightly over his mouth. He clenched his teeth, which were numb from the constant pressure that lay against them, and drew in air from the gap that opened up at the side of the gag.

Burberry went through his mental list, again. He knew exactly where the instep of the man's right foot was positioned and also his groin and wind pipe. He had rehearsed half a dozen blows to disable him. He was ready for any opportunity, whenever it should present itself.

There was a tiny creak on the stairs beyond the open door to their left. The man restraining Burberry made the faintest rumble in his throat as a caution to remain quiet. Burberry could feel his own heartbeat thudding rapidly in his neck and the accompanying noise of his pulse in his ears became deafening. A full minute passed and there was no further noise from the stairs. The man slackened his grip and relaxed his posture a little.

The soldier on the stairs froze and opened his mouth wide, as if catching flies. His gaping mouth served to prevent his breathing from being audible. He had ever so gently put his weight forward on his foot and this had elicited an unexpected creak from the stair beneath it. Now, with the moment gone, he slowly closed his mouth and tried to inhale and exhale at a normal pace. He prayed for his comrades, downstairs, to go back to stomping around and talking loudly. Their sudden pause in activity had come at exactly the wrong moment. As if they could hear his wishes, there was a sudden rumpus from the ground floor and several raised voices. He quickly took advantage and nimbly made the last two steps onto the landing.

Burberry felt the McCarthy man tense, again, as if he had heard something. Burberry was absolutely certain that there had been nothing discernible. He now became irrationally worried whether this man had some kind of evil sixth sense.

The constable closed his eyes and tried to concentrate. This, he reflected, was a dire situation! These might be his last moments. The McCarthys had become unaccountably worried, just before what turned out to be the launch of an attack. Two of them had bundled him upstairs. When the shouting and firing had begun, downstairs, one of the two had gone out onto the landing and had never returned. From the sound of it, he had been shot by someone in the hall below. His cry of alarm had been followed by a thud and clatter, which suggested that he had fallen part way down the stairs. His subsequent moans and groans had got weaker and more muffled, over a period of minutes, and soon after that, they had stopped and never resumed.

Burberry felt the man behind him change position. Suddenly, the pressure of the pistol against his temple disappeared, but a second later, he felt it pressing up under his chin, forcing him to lift his head to accommodate it. The McCarthy leaned to one side and seemed to fumble for something, in a pocket or bag, with his free hand. A few moments later he felt cold steel on his cheek. The McCarthy pressed his lips against Burberry's ear.

"I'm going to cut your gag off," the man mumbled in his ear, "But if you speak even one word, other than what I tell you to say, I will blow your head off your shoulders. Nod if you understand."

Much to the McCarthy's irritation, and without intending to do it, the constable made the tiniest snort. He felt the McCarthy clench his teeth and, even without being able to see his face, he knew that his captor had a puzzled expression.

After a second or two, the muzzle of the pistol dropped down an inch, allowing Burberry's head to move slightly and giving him the physical space to nod. He obligingly nodded.

After a slight pause, he felt the blade of the knife glide up his cheek and the gag fell away. Having had difficulty in breathing, Burberry took in a deep lung full of air. The McCarthy – unappreciative of the noise – made another threatening growl in his ear.

The soldier, standing with his back flat against the wall, next to the doorway, heard everything. The McCarthy, blessed with the instincts of a wolf, seemed to know that he was there.

Just as Burberry got his breathing back under control, he felt a sudden stillness envelop him. The room seemed to become oddly quiet. He could still hear the soldiers, downstairs, and the McCarthy beside him, but everything took on a distant quality. An instant later, he was bathed in a pale orange light that seemed to emanate from a cloud that had gathered around him.

"Say **only** what I tell you to say," the McCarthy hissed in his ear, "And don't try anything stupid or brave."

The man moved his face away from Burberry's ear, while he considered his next words. The constable turned his head slightly to the side and felt the muscles of his eyeballs tug in protest as he looked as far out of the corner of his eyes as he possibly could. Burberry could just make out that the man was screwing up his eyes against the dark. He was straining to see across into the doorway. Burberry was astonished to comprehend what this meant. The man could not see the illumination of the orange glow! For him, it was still almost total darkness with only the vaguest glimmer of light penetrating from the outside.

CHAPTER 12

"This is going to sound strange, Hamish, but I need to say it out loud," Alex ventured.

Hamish grunted to encourage him to continue.

"I can see something. It's like an orange glow, inside the room, like a firefly. I'm guessing that it isn't really there. Am I right?"

"I was just thinking the same thing, myself," Hamish replied, "I suppose if we're able to see it, then we are meant to be able to see it."

"By whatever force or influence...."

The two men returned to their silent study of the distant scene through the magnifying lenses of their muskets.

"That's Constable Burberry." Alex suggested, tentatively, "He is standing in front of somebody. I can see their head over his shoulder."

Hamish grunted his agreement.

"They are too close together to hit one without risking hitting the other," Alex noted, then – realising the overwhelming obviousness of the situation – he apologised, "Sorry."

"The orange glow is like the light from an invisible lantern," Hamish mused, "But it only shines for an arm's length, then it fades."

"I'll tell you what," Alex murmured, speaking half to himself, "I could always just close my eyes and squeeze the trigger when it feels like the right moment."

"Don't you dare!" Hamish snapped.

Alex fixed Hamish with a devilish grin and they both laughed at his absurdity.

CHAPTER 13

Queen Annis – the nineteen year old Queen of the West – took a deep breath, clenched her jaw and reached up to pull down the smaller of the two visors on her helmet.

It had been a small thing that she had done that morning, she reflected. She had walked a short distance along the far bank of the River Spey. It was a ritual that her forebears had performed, every five years, for the last eight centuries. Though a small thing, its significance was overwhelming. It was a public assertion of the boundary of her royal territory and, as such, it was a calculated provocation.

This year, there had been rumours of possible conflict. The Chieftain of the Clan MacDonald had become so concerned for her safety that he had sent a sizeable army to bolster her own. Additionally, he had taken the bold step of providing her with an Honour Guard.

While Honour Guards had, at one time, been a regular spectacle, their use had diminished over the years. An Honour Guard was always comprised of the very best fighters available. Despite being clad in highly polished and flamboyantly decorative armour, they were an elite squad and were an extremely potent and lethal force.

The much feared bloody clash with Clan Grant had never happened. Instead, in an astonishing turn of events, their eight centuries long feud with the Queens of the West had been unexpectedly resolved and they had pledged their swords to her.

The Clan Grant bagpipes had wailed an alarm as the neighbouring Clan Rose had begun a sudden attack on her forces. On hearing them, Gavin Crombie, her First Office, and Balgair McRory, the Captain of her Honour Guard, had slewed their horses around, throwing up a shower of grass and mud, and had spurred them towards her.

Seconds later, the Laird Grant's outriders came galloping up to her with The Grant himself between them.

Annis beamed at him. Now that the Clan Grant accepted that Queen Kiffan had always been their ally and *never* their enemy, their zeal and fervour would serve well to thwart her treacherous enemies, the Campbells.

"I am a warrior queen," Annis shouted to them, at the top of her voice, "From a line of warrior queens, and this day I will do as all who have come before me have done."

In reply, there were cheers, the rattling of swords against shields and the slapping of gauntleted hands against steel clad thighs.

"I will grip my sword," she declared, "And I will kill my enemies!"

The shouts and cheers, in response, were loud and fervent.

Annis thought wistfully of 'Kiffan the Defiant', the first of her line, who – at the very same age of nineteen – had taken up arms against the Viking invaders of Scotland. She wondered how terrified she must have felt. She wondered how daunted she must have been. She wondered how she had managed to muster such courage.

"To battle!" She cried, holding up her sword.

She urged her horse forward and, immediately, her Honour Guard formed up around her as a wedge, like an arrowhead. Without another word, she set off towards the gap in her enemy's front line and into the maelstrom beyond it. The Laird Grant did not hesitate. He and his group of riders followed her through the gap.

Queen Annis could not suppress a smile. The Clan Grant had, little more than an hour ago, been her sworn enemy. How ironic, she noted, that fate should seek to test their new allegiance so promptly and with such little delay!

The Queen, much to her clear and vocal annoyance, was steered off to the left by her overprotective escort, drawing a blistering reprimand from her.

Not far away, an aggressive band of her enemy was moving wide in an attempt to outflank her archers who, with their quivers empty, had begun to press in on them with their swords drawn. Annis wheeled her horse around to circle around a grassy hummock to take the attackers head-on.

Reaching down from her saddle, Annis caught the first marauder in the face with her sword. As he slumped to the ground, she parried a blow from the man behind him before bringing her sword down on his shoulder, shearing his arm clean away. The move was so incredibly fast, her victim was left to stare in amazement.

It was as if Annis and her horse were one. Her mount responded with such quick and sure compliance to her gentlest touch that it seemed to be an extension of her own body.

She swerved around a man with an axe and split the back of his head with a rearward stroke of her blade. Next, she took down a man with a scythe followed by a man wielding a spiked ball on a chain. Another three fell in quick succession, before a fourth managed to dive below her reach.

Seeing her approach, a man ahead of her veered in her direction, slashing back and forth with his sword in a whirling pattern to intercept her horse. Annis pressed her knee against the side of her steed and it leaned and began to turn away. It was too late. The man's sword carved through the air on a course to strike the side of her horse's head. Leaning forward, Annis raised her foot to kick the man's arm and simultaneously struck down, hard, with her sword. She knew that if she failed to make contact, it would almost certainly mean slicing into her own leg.

There was a clang of steel and Annis felt the jarring shock of the impact as her sword hit the cross piece of her adversary's sword, only narrowly missing his blade. The sensation travelled from her wrist to her elbow like a bolt of lightning. Deflected by the collision, the man's weapon was turned aside. A split second later, her foot struck the man's elbow, breaking his arm.

A grey blur came from out of her vision to her right in a daring attack. In an instant, the man disappeared under Balgair's horse as he deliberately rode it over him.

The MacDonald and McRory archers continued their assault on the men in the enemy's flank. The flurry of claymores, axes and spears, clashed repeatedly in the air with the accompanying chime of metal on metal. The shouts and screams turned into a background thrum of incoherent babble, punctuated by random cries of gleeful victory or of mortal anguish.

A little way ahead, one of her riders was being brought down as his horse was struck on its head by a wooden hammer on a pole. Annis promptly pulled her own horse to a stop, the beast's hooves hurling up soil as it scrabbled for purchase. Grabbing her larger, heavier battle sword, Annis jumped down from her saddle. In two long strides she reached the fallen horseman, taking his assailant by surprise. With a lunging strike she pierced through the man's chest, from front to back, and then kicked him in the belly. Drawing out her sword, she twirled around to bring the blade back up, over, then down again. The manoeuvre allowed her to strike a second man above his ear, cutting his jaw from his skull, and severing half way through his neck.

Annis reached down and grabbed the dazed cavalry rider by the back of his tunic. Placing her foot against the saddle of his horse, she cried out with the effort as she hauled him backwards, dragging his leg from under his mount.

Looking up, she found a man running towards her with a pitchfork. She dodged his thrust just as two of her Honour Guards pounded up on horseback, one either side of her, knocking the fork from the man's hands before simultaneously skewering him either side of his chest with their swords.

Another of her Honour Guards grabbed her by the arm and hauled her off her feet, landing her with a smack against the side of her horse. Annis twisted around and pulled herself up into her saddle.

In the midst of the pandemonium, another Honour Guard commanded his steed to hunker onto its haunches and, as it did so, he reached down and took hold of his fallen comrade. With a tremendous yank, the momentum exaggerated as his horse stood up, he lifted the man from the ground and propelled him across the back of another rider's horse. That rider reached around behind his saddle and gripped his passenger's belt, before digging in his spurs and speeding away.

The distraction had attracted some unwanted attention and, in response, Annis whirled her horse about and charged down two of the opposing army who were heading in their direction from out of the crowd. Then, taking up her lighter sword, she fatally slashed and cut another who tried to pick up the fallen pole-hammer.

The two McRory Honour Guards closest to Annis — apparently fearing for her safety — hastened to her. Within moments, Balgair appeared and did the same. Undaunted by events, she led their group of four as they used their horses to push and barge their way into the side of the throng. As if working cattle, they succeeded in separating away half a dozen enemy soldiers. These, they despatched savagely and without mercy, Annis managing to decapitate one of them in the process.

Balgair shouted a warning to Annis. She looked around and, with a start, realised that a large force was coming at them from behind. Around thirty men, who had been crouched out of sight beyond the grassy hummock, had sprung to their feet and were now attacking from around it. Annis knew, instinctively, that this force meant to take her.

Two other Honour Guards, easily distinguishable by their bronzed helmets, emerged from the clamour nearby, fighting their way out with grim urgency, and took up protective positions.

Balgair urged his horse forward. Annis and the others followed. Her guards, she noted, fought with a fury that was daunting to behold. They seemed like men possessed! Three of their number pushed their way into the midst of the approaching force, which opened up a little too easily for the queen's liking. On emerging through the other side, they discovered another line of enemy soldiers had formed ahead of them.

Suddenly, they found themselves surrounded.

CHAPTER 14

The McRory horsemen shouted a command and their horses, three in a line, rose up into the air in a leap that brought them crashing down full square on top of the enemy. The horses scrambled to regain their balance, crushing the attackers under hoof in the effort.

The riders gave their steeds another command and, in answer, the creatures reared up on their back legs and appeared to dance in the air with their front hooves, caving in the heads and chests and shattering the arms and shoulders of their startled opponents.

Balgair took out a whistle and began to blow it, making a shrill, high-pitched note that cut the air. This plaintive note was picked up by the riders around them on their own whistles. Within a few seconds, the piercing whine had risen to a crescendo.

Across the meadow the ears of the horses, at all points on the battlefield, pricked up and the air resonated to their answering shrieks and whinnies. Since they were foals, still sucking milk from their mothers, the sound of the whistle had been the summons they had learned must neither be ignored nor delayed. The MacDonald foot soldiers, in the thick of the conflict, hastily sprang away from the cavalry horses, desperately urging their Grants allies to do the same.

Within moments of the first notes, there had been a colossal surge of activity right the way across the churning mob of combatants. Now – like the progress of a mounting tidal wave – over twenty riders came bolting out from the midst of the horde. Enemy warriors were flung aside, like soil being turned by a plough, as the stampede emerged with explosive force. They tore headlong into the enemy raiding party that was surrounding Annis, battering them to the ground and trampling them under hoof.

The horses skidded to a halt in a rolling wave of splattering mud, then careered around, frantically grappling for traction, before hurling themselves back the way they had come. Their eyes bulged, their nostrils flared, their ears flapped and they bared their teeth as they dashed the writhing mass of wounded and broken bodies beneath their hooves.

Gripped by a common frenzy – an instinct to defend both their equine and human herd – these loving, tender creatures had been transformed into blood lusting devils.

Seeing the horror on the face of his queen, Balgair came alongside her.

"What have I just witnessed?" She shouted to him above the noise.

"In answer to the distress whistles," Balgair bellowed, "The horses regard the sight of their riders in distress as no different to seeing their own foals being set upon by a pack of wolves."

Those cavalrymen who had dismounted to take up hand to hand combat with the remaining force, now climbed back into their saddles, the epic struggle having been concluded.

Annis' horsemen had sustained a range of injuries, but were almost all able to fight on and were heading back to the main throng when a mounted McRory officer appeared, galloping down the field towards them.

The newcomer saluted Balgair and bowed to Annis, as Sachairi rode to meet him.

At Balgair's insistence, they left the field of battle to take up position beneath a line of trees.

Sachairi and the rider who had arrived came to join them. The rider threw himself into an animated discussion and repeatedly gestured through the trees towards the river.

Despite being unable to distinguish what was being said, Annis could, none-the-less, understand the portent of the discussion. There was trouble on the other side of the river.

Presently, Sachairi returned to announce the bad news.

While she had been fighting with the Clan Rose, her main force across the river had been under attack from the Campbells. The conflict was hanging in the balance. The situation called for reinforcements.

The fight on her own side of the river had peaked and begun to wane. It could now be contained, her officers agreed, without further need of mounted troops.

Balgair announced that he would take their cavalry across the Spey to help.

Taking as many archers as had survived, Balgair gathered the riders into two columns. Annis ran her eye down the assembled lines and her heart sank as she saw their depleted numbers.

"How many have we lost?" Annis asked.

"It is hard to tell, but it looks like we have lost around six cavalrymen and at least ten bowmen," Balgair replied.

"We have lost something like half of our thirty foot soldiers," Gavin added, appearing at her side.

Her heart ached for the wives, the sisters, the children and the parents who were yet to hear of their loss, back on the West Coast in the MacDonald homelands.

"I'm going with you across the Spey," Annis announced.

Balgair, Sachairi and Gavin all looked genuinely shocked.

"Your Majesty," Gavin urged, "You have faced enough danger already and nobody – but **nobody** – could say that you have not given a good account of yourself!"

"You have horses with saddles and no riders." Annis responded, waving a hand towards the mounted force, "You have gaps with neither rider nor horse. There are bows and swords without their owners. "

The three officers, who already knew this only too well, obediently turned to look for themselves and their faces were heartbreakingly sad.

"There are widows and orphans who waved off their brave men to war who will never see them again," Annis declared, "They will never feel their kiss or their touch. They will never hear their voices. They will never see their faces. I will not cower from our enemy when these men have shown such courage and made such a sacrifice."

Sachairi looked to Balgair. Balgair looked to Gavin. Gavin shook his head and held up his hands.

"Her mother was stubborn like this," Gavin told them, "And she was as brave as anybody I have ever met in my life."

Balgair was silent for a long moment before he spoke.

"If I were to return to The MacDonald…."

He let his words hang, knowing that there was no need to finish his sentence.

CHAPTER 15

Reluctantly, Balgair left Sachairi to conclude the battle and set off for the river with Annis and Gavin behind him.

"Eight centuries ago," Gavin announced, to the cavalry riders in their column, "The Vikings came to Scotland to plunder and spoil. Even the bravest of men trembled. It was a woman who led the army that opposed them. It was The Queen of the West. The Campbells have little idea what awaits them. Let's go and give them a taste of what it is to cross her!"

There was a cheer and a shout from the men as they called out their agreement.

"Then it's decided," said Annis, firmly.

Their party rode across the river and up the bank and ascended the hill to the forest, where they gathered in the trees to discuss the battle ahead of them.

They were at the top of a huge meadow that ran down a gradual hill to a stream at its base. On the far side of the stream was a steep hill, leading to a rocky outcrop near its peak. On the near side of the stream, up the middle of the meadow, was a gulley. The gulley was shallow and wide at its lower end, where it met the water, but its sides became increasingly steep until it became treacherous and uncrossable at its upper reaches. It ended in a sheer rock face, along the edge of the forest, below them, where the trees had grown out over the drop, leaning precariously into the void.

On the opposite bank of the gulley, at the middle point between the stream and the forest, the MacDonald and Brydda forces were ferociously locked in battle with their attackers. Despite being outnumbered, they appeared to be just about holding their own. Despite fighting uphill, it seemed they preferred to have the gulley to their back and had little concern for the risk of being forced into it.

The McRory cavalry was despatched to head further up through the forest trail to the ridge that lay out of view at the top of the hill. Their mission was to cross the pack mule route along the rocky summit and then descend, again, to take the enemy from the rear.

Balgair shouted instructions to his foot soldiers and they ran to the top of the gulley and began pushing their way through the dense tangle of vegetation at the base of the trees. This route would ultimately allow them to come around the back of their foes to join in the attack of their mounted troops.

Annis spurred her horse and galloped out from the cover of the trees and pulled her horse up a little way down the incline. The animal snorted and neighed as it came to a halt, its hooves sinking into the mud beneath the sparse grass. Gavin, Balgair and her Honour Guard rode out beside her.

"The enemy has reinforcements coming across the top edge of the far field beyond the stream," Balgair observed, "They will be trying to get around behind us. Our archers have replenished their arrows. If we can get them to the bottom of the hill, we can see how many of the enemy they can take down."

"Will they hit them, from that distance?" Annis asked, dubiously.

"**These** men with **these** bows certainly will!" Balgair assured her with more than a hint of pride in his voice.

With this, the archers were duly despatched to race down the slope to the bank of the stream. From there, they set about unleashing wave after wave of arrows that curved up into the air and swooped down into the midst of the arriving soldiers. The further their adversaries advanced, the closer they got within range. The effect of this was to stop them in their tracks and force them to retreat.

After regrouping, it soon became clear that the enemy force was going to go back the way they had come. Their intention was clearly to circle back up the far side of the meadow – out of range of archers – and attempt to take the MacDonald troops from their flank.

Balgair signalled for his archers to come back up the hill and sent them across to the near side of the gulley to fire at the main body of the Campbells from there.

Queen Annis rode hard down the hill, to the bottom of the gulley, which had just been vacated by their archers. Her mare picked its way across the rock-strewn gulley with astounding agility. Gavin and Balgair followed close in her wake with her Honour Guard in tight pursuit. The steepness of the far bank of the stream, now over to their left, prevented anybody from approaching them directly from that direction.

They watched as their opponent's reinforcing troops, recently repelled by McRory arrow fire, filed down to the bottom of the far hill and began to cross the stream further up.

Looking up the slope, Annis and her party saw that the battle seemed to be turning against the MacDonald forces. They appeared to have been compelled to give ground. Balgair's heart sank as he realised that their advantage might be lost if they waited for their cavalry to appear from the top. Those riders would, by now, have all dismounted and would be carefully leading their horses across the slippery piles of shifting rocks and loose scree beyond the forest.

Annis turned her horse and came alongside Gavin and Balgair.

"Their reinforcements are large in number," She observed, "There will soon be two of them for every MacDonald soldier, despite the work of our archers."

"We are in very real danger," agreed Gavin.

"We need to ride up yonder," Annis asserted, sweeping her hand through the air to show the intended route, "We must clash with them before they can take our main troops from their flank and push them into the gulley."

"I agree," replied Balgair, "If we put ourselves between the two forces, and remain mobile, we can likely reduce the risk of it."

"You're right," Gavin agreed, "We need to harass and delay them as best we can, but if they can get enough troops up the slope, we risk being cut off."

"We need to hold on until our reserve MacDonald force arrives," Balgair told them, "Word has gone to them to march. They will be happy to know that they'll be fighting Campbells instead of Grants!"

"The best way for us to drive home an attack," Annis declared, "Would be to ride uphill, ahead of our enemy, then come around and attack them by riding back downhill."

"We will be able to zig zag back and forth through their leading ranks," Balgair enthused, "To blunt their progress, but – we being a small force – that won't be without risk."

"It will buy valuable time, though," Gavin conceded, reluctantly.

Balgair grunted his irritation and scowled at his companions. Annis looked at him, levelly, and spoke in a flat, measured tone.

"Speak your mind."

"My Queen," Balgair replied, "You ride into battle with your Honour Guard as if they were a fighting unit of your horsemen, rather than your close escort for your personal protection. I am accountable to The MacDonald and this was not their intended purpose. I would not wish to incur his wrath!"

"You would rather incur **my** wrath?" Annis replied, disdainfully, "Perhaps The MacDonald has mistaken what sort of queen I am! For it is not the tradition of my family to stand and watch while others fight!"

Her Honour Guard straightened themselves in their saddles and sat tall and defiant with their chins out and their shoulders back. Balgair narrowed his eyes at them and allowed his scowl to deepen. He was aware that they were silently siding with her. He was, also, only too aware that they were being increasingly drawn to and seduced by the reckless courage of this young woman. He was further aware of how they seemed to bristle with pride in her.

Balgair sensed the drama of the moment and the momentous significance of it. He allowed the tension to hang, undissipated, and it hovered like a hawk suspended in the air. As if to add to the misery of the moment, a thin rain began to fall. It was cold and dreary and splashed without enthusiasm. The grass quickly started to squelch under foot.

The yoke of The MacDonald's expectations weighed heavily on Balgair's shoulders. He soberly contemplated the very real danger that would ensue for him if there were to be a disaster, here, today. The MacDonald was a brave man, a proud man and a man of principal. Balgair considered his options and decided that he would speak with the same note of defiance as his master.

"Your mother would be proud of you," he said.

Annis, foreseeing the beginning of a lecture, struck her fist against her armour, landing it over her heart, and then repeated the gesture with her fingers spread in a claw. She paused a moment and then thrust forward her hand towards her Honour Guard, her fingers gripping the air like an eagle's claw.

"Aon chridhe!" She cried, this being the Gaelic for "One heart".

Her escort shouted back the same.

"Aon adhbhar!" She cried, this being the Gaelic for "One purpose".

Her escort shouted back the same.

"Aon anam!" She cried, this being the Gaelic for "One soul".

Her escort shouted back the same.

With a suddenness that took both Gavin and Balgair by surprise, Annis spurred her horse and galloped away up the field, a shower of mud and dirt in her wake, with her Honour Guard bounding after her, close on her heels.

Catching him just at the point of moving off, Gavin turned to Balgair and delayed him.

"I cannot tell, for sure, what effect she has on her enemies," Gavin confided, "But I swear she puts the fear of God into me!"

They both laughed a bitter and ironic laugh and took off after the other horsemen.

Balgair reflected on the convenience of those monarchs who drew scorn and derision by always staying far away from the battlefield. Faint hearted they might be, he mused, but far and away less challenging to keep safe!

"These are Campbell men," Balgair called to Gavin, "For while they carry no banners and their tartans are varied and none of them particular, they have the smell of Campbells about them!"

"Aye," Gavin agreed, "They are Campbells or else they are the simpering dogs of the Campbells."

Satisfied that she was a sufficient way up the shallow slope, Annis leaned over in her saddle and urged her steed around in a sharp turn, throwing up a spectacular wave of turf and soil. Her guards wheeled around with her, their horses chewing up the meadow in similar fashion. Presently, they were in full charge downhill, on a line for head-on collision with the Campbell troops who were coming up towards them.

The queen's escort applied the briefest hint of their spurs and caught up with her, taking up position to ride eight abreast. Within a few strides, Gavin and Balgair were there, too, now making their formation a line of ten.

"You three, break out with me to the right!" Bellowed Balgair to the riders at his end of the line.

"You three, break out with me to the left!" Yelled Gavin to the riders at the opposite end.

"Break and swing around to take them from the flanks!" Balgair ordered.

At this, the two outer groups of four drifted away to either side and began a wide arc that would intersect the approaching enemy at two points behind the leaders of their column. The leaders, themselves, had the queen and her nearest cavalryman to contend with.

At first, the approaching fighters continued to march resolutely and defiantly up the meadow, a line of men arranged three wide and showing no sign of being flustered. As the cavalry neared them, the splattering drum of hoofbeats on the ground and the snorting of their steeds, appeared to abruptly unnerve them.

At fifteen paces, a dozen men at the front scattered, left and right, in wild panic. The troops behind them, suddenly able to see the approaching riders for the first time, were next to break rank. Annis and her companions ploughed into them, like a pair of boulders rolling down a mountain. The riders and their horses trampled, toppled and tumbled into the soldiers. The armour on the horses' chests, upper legs, knees and shins clanged and rang like gongs as they made contact with the swords, shields and helmets of their prey.

A little way down, wheeling around to come from the left, Gavin and his group of riders ploughed their beasts into the side of the soldiers. Their line of attack impacted at a shallow angle to maximise the chaos and injury they delivered. Some of their victims had had time to draw their swords and raise their shields, but their efforts were more or less useless against the four-legged battering rams that pounded into them.

A short way beyond, this time off to the right, Balgair and his cluster of cavalry riders crashed into the column of soldiers from the opposite side, knocking them down like skittle pins and throwing them in every direction. Swords were swung, but with little effect, and their shields were tossed up into the air to spin like cartwheels down the field or embed into the grass on their edges.

The McRory riders brought their horses out of the throng, whirled them around and charged them back in again. The riders cut, slashed, and spun, this way and that, to maintain the advantage. Despite this, the jostling confusion of their enemy at the start of the conflict slowly began to form into something more organised.

At the shouting and braying of their leader, the Campbell reinforcements began coming forward and locking shields into a wall to contain the horses. This would normally have been less of a problem – as a heavy horse can usually batter its way through such an obstacle – but the ground was becoming so churned up and muddy that the horses were finding it hard to keep from sliding.

Balgair spotted the brewing danger and called out a warning. Safe within the confines of the slippery mud pan, the Campbell soldiers started bringing forward their spears and halberds. Annis and her men, it seemed, were about to be pinned down between the newcomers and the main battle.

CHAPTER 16

Janine pondered Mister Chang's words.

'We could think of no better way to hide you from others than to hide you from yourself,' he had said.

She concluded that she had been well and truly hidden, indeed. She looked around at the eager, loyal faces of her supporters. They were filled with concern.

"Mister Chang," said Janine, "I remember you well, but – then again – I don't remember you at all. It is a strange dilemma, since I don't even recall how much I know about you or when it was that I knew you."

Mister Chang bowed and embarked on an explanation.

"I was born and raised in China. It was my home for over thirty years. I served as an apprentice to three different masters. I learned from each of these wise men. From one, I learned the ancient arts of combat. From another, I learned the mystical arts of herbal medicine. From the third, I learned the skill of understanding and controlling the human mind. Over many years I built up my knowledge and perfected the skills they taught me until I, too, became a master.

"I was held in high esteem by the Provincial Governor and, after proving my worth on many occasions, he recommended me for a position in the Emperor's Court. I was to be an assistant to a Minister. On my way there, a journey of several weeks, the caravan with which I was travelling was attacked by bandits. I was forced to defend myself and the merchant who conveyed me.

"During the fight that ensued, I killed several of the attackers. One in particular was the leader of the force. He was a man in splendid armour and, it was plain to see, someone of high birth. He turned out to be the Emperor's nephew. He was raising funds to conduct a war against the Emperor's foes and regarded stealing from merchants as an acceptable method. I was forced to flee for my life. Retribution by the crown was guaranteed to be terrible and cruel, and their search for me would be relentless.

"By some stroke of luck, I evaded capture and made it as far as a port. There I hid on a supply boat that was going out to meet an ocean-going vessel in the bay with provisions. That vessel was 'The Highland Spirit', a ship belonging to The Duke of Bo'Ness. I stowed myself away onboard. When the crew discovered me, I expected to be beaten savagely and tossed overboard for the sharks. Instead, to my astonishment, they dressed my wounds, they gave me water and they fed me.

"I had always believed that Europeans were wild, untamed animals. For that slur I apologise to you all. My opinion was the product of ignorance and prejudice. I was shocked and stunned to discover that the captain and his officers spoke good Mandarin. I was intrigued to find that they wanted to know my story.

"I told them my tale, but − as a precaution − I reduced the ranks of the robbers to be no more than a local nobleman waylaying merchants with the help of a rogue gang of mercenaries. They listened patiently to me until my explanation was complete. Then, they began to ask me questions. When they learned of my abilities in the healing arts, I was immediately appointed as the physician to their fleet of three ships.

"I had a keen interest in literature and had read both classical and general writings on a wide variety of topics. I knew, from this, that if I remained in China, my chances of evading arrest by the Emperor's troops would be close to zero. In light of this, the role of a healer aboard a ship compared very favourably to that of a condemned man in a prison cell, awaiting execution!

"By this method of employment, I paid for my passage on the high seas and found myself, one day, in the port of Ardrossan in Scotland. We arrived in the middle of the night. The weather was cold, wet and windy. This, I was told, was typical Scottish weather and the truth of that has not, since, been called into doubt!"

Mister Chang's audience laughed politely.

"Even with my limited knowledge of Scotland, I thought it was strange to arrive at Ardrossan rather than somewhere like Glasgow. I thought it stranger still that we should be risking the perils of navigation on a moonless night with all of the ship's lanterns extinguished. I soon learned the reason for this odd behaviour. Not all of our cargo was intended to arrive through official channels. As soon as we tied up, we were mobbed by a swarm of hand carts and little wagons that took away many of the bolts of silk and casks of spirits we were carrying.

"I was allowed to roam our vessel freely and was able to observe a couple of more sizeable wagons arrive on the dock that were drawn by large, strong, well fed horses. These vehicles were operated by men in mysterious long, dark capes. These capes would flutter in the wind, from time to time, to reveal the black, grey and dark blue livery of uniforms that were fastened with gleaming brass buttons. The posture, gait and overall deportment of these men was very particular and, at times, assertive. I did not need to be told that these were military men. The scene did not take a lot of working out. It was clear that here in Scotland, as in China and the world over, government officials were willing to look the other way and ignore what was going on, if they were given the right inducement.

"I had learned a fair amount of Gaelic from the crew, who thought that my attempts at pronouncing their native language were hilarious. My errors provided them with endless entertainment on the voyage. It was a comedy of which they never tired. This was much to my benefit and I exploited it ruthlessly to learn still more.

"The officers aboard the ship were more formal and showed greater restraint in their endeavours to teach me their own preferred language, which turned out to be English. I soon realised that English was a language that these men employed to talk in secret, over the heads of the crew. This was mostly done when they had bad news to discuss between themselves. That news would either be disheartening or something that risked feeding the sailors' many superstitions.

"Believe me when I say that the sailors had a superstition to cover every possible occasion! They held them as dear and true – and observed them as rigidly – as any religion!

"After setting sail from Ardrossan – our ship noticeably lighter – we made the short journey up the coast to Glasgow. This leg of our journey saw all of the lanterns on our decks lit, once more. At Glasgow, our arrival soon attracted the attention of people whom I later learned to be Customs Officers. As they came aboard, our Captain greeted the three of them with cordial familiarity and each discretely accepted a small purse. These cloth bags – which clinked softly with the sound of coins – were declared to be *'in appreciation of their hard work for the king.'* I was fairly certain that the king was unlikely to see any of the contents.

"Our cargo was unloaded, this time less hastily and more methodically. The work was done by a group of dock workers who appeared sullenly resigned to the drizzle and blustery winds. As they busied themselves, we descended a walkway and climbed into a carriage that was waiting for us. I was ushered to follow the captain and his officers and was grateful to be out of the dismal weather. The carriage stopped at several inns, dropping off members of the senior crew at each, but my moment to alight never came and I was eventually the only other occupant of the coach other than the captain.

"My skills and knowledge appeared to have elevated me in status beyond my actual rank of fleet healer. The truth of this became even clearer when the captain announced that I was to accompany him, the following day, to somewhere called 'Brech Woorlach' to meet The Duke of Bo'Ness. I had no idea who he might be, but I gathered that he must be an important person of rank and that to be introduced to him was a privilege."

Mister Chang looked remorsefully at The Duke, who returned a good natured smile and shrugged his shoulders.

"Brech Woorlach already had a healer. She was a good one, too – considering the knowledge and traditions of the time – and was well familiar with an impressive range of herbs and medicinal flora and fungi. The expertise that was required of me, I was soon to discover, was not simply the healing of the body. They wished to avail themselves of my knowledge of healing and controlling the mind."

Mister Chang stood up and, after sighing a deep, long sigh, he bowed low to Janine.

"It is at this point, Your Majesty, that I must offer you my most profound and heartfelt apologies, for it is due to my actions that you find yourself in the distressing, disturbing and very confusing situation that you do. It was I who delivered a resolution to an extremely vexing and dangerous set of circumstances that had befallen your family. Those times were perilous and unpredictable for everyone, but especially for those who were not solely, singularly and exclusively committed to the support of the King of Scotland."

Janine gave a tight lipped smile of acceptance.

"In 1603 – the year you were born – King James of Scotland inherited the English throne and became King James of England. There were all kinds of groups and factions struggling for influence and competing to show their credentials as loyal subjects. One thing that was overwhelmingly unacceptable – and very likely to get a person killed – was believing in the old ways of the Highlands.

"The most dangerous belief, amongst these, was the upholding of the true and rightful sovereignty of the Queen of the West. Such followers were hunted down and exterminated. Scotland, they would have everyone believe, had a brave new future with England. There were even those with aspirations to unite the two parliaments to bring about a single nation. Old 'superstitions' about a warrior queen were wholly unwelcome and regarded as treason."

Mister Chang, who had begun to pace back and forth in front of the fire, was now wringing his hands and frowning at his recollections.

"The current Duke of Bo'Ness is as completely loyal to the Queen of the West as was his father.

"His father became a believer upon his first encounter with the, then, holder of that title, 'Queen of the West.' It was on the fateful day that he was washed up, half dead, on a Scottish beach.

"He believed that her love of the poor was a true reflection of what God expects of mankind and that her kindness and charity were the embodiment of biblical teachings. His success, and resulting wealth, did nothing to dilute that belief. As both a rich merchant and, later, as The Duke of Bo'Ness, his allegiance never wavered."

Everybody sat in rapt silence, completely captivated by his story.

"The woman he met that day – The Queen of the West – was, of course, your mother, Your Majesty."

Janine looked shocked and stunned.

"My mother?" She asked, his assertion taking her completely by surprise.

"Yes, Your Majesty, your mother when she was very young," Mister Chang confirmed.

"When you were born, despite everyone's best efforts to keep your existence a secret, word of you eventually spread. It was inevitable that this news would reach the ears of your family's enemies. As a result, it wasn't long before an attempt was made on your mother's life and, subsequently, on your own.

"Ever since James had been declared King of Scotland, back in 1567, things had become risky, but the situation began to grow steadily worse with every year that passed. The use of Brech Woorlach was changed to include activities above and beyond those of being the seat of a duke and duchess."

Mister Chang looked at Francesca, enquiringly. Francesca nodded. Janine knew, straight away, the nature of their silent conversation. It was confirmation that Janine was already fully aware.

"I presume," Janine said, locking eyes with Mister Chang, "That we are not merely talking about it becoming an orphanage?"

"No, Your Majesty," replied Mister Chang, partially suppressing an impish smile, "We are not."

Mister Chang bowed to Janine and then continued.

"The Duke established a secret school for the training of spies."

CHAPTER 17

Janine blinked at the directness of Mister Chang's revelation.

"It had become very clear to The Duke," Mister Chang resumed, "That spies were being actively used against him by governments both in Scotland and England and by their friends abroad.

"The Duke made it widely known that he was doing no more than training servants who could be relied upon to be loyal to him and his allies. This was only half the truth.

"It was common knowledge that, all across society, everybody's opponents were gathering any kind of information on them that they possibly could. Nobody was in any doubt that much of this information was being obtained by dubious means."

The Duke and The Duchess both nodded, solemnly, at the memory.

"We — for I had become a willing accomplice in the matter — took our mission to defend you, Your Majesty, as our life's calling. Within a year, we had moved our secret school above and beyond its original purpose."

Suddenly Francesca sat bolt upright and Janine was puzzled to see that she was looking desperately at Mister Chang. As she did so, she shook her head as discretely as she could.

Mister Chang arched an eyebrow at Francesca, then looked to The Duke, evidently seeking permission for something. The Duke slowly nodded. Mister Chang bowed to him before giving Francesca a wistful and apologetic smile.

"It is said," Mister Chang declared, holding up both palms to the ceiling in a gesture of helplessness, "That when needs must, the Devil drives, Your Majesty."

Janine cocked her head at Mister Chang and, from the corner of her eye, saw Francesca lower hers.

"As a young man in China, while I developed an extensive range of combat skills – becoming as fearsome an opponent with my bare hands as most were with a weapon – I also delved deeper into the dark side of the martial arts.

"I learned, sharpened and perfected the learnings of those who did not simply live outside the law, but beyond the moral code of most societies. I studied hard to hone that learning to the point of expertise and mastery."

Francesca looked up and turned to Janine, tears brimming in her eyes, and gave her a look of pain and regret.

"I began to train our students," Mister Chang continued, "To be the most exemplary and highly skilled assassins."

Janine's eyes widened and Francesca bit the corner of her lip.

"A significant percentage of the servants you see here are trained killers," Mister Chang explained, "They are accomplished in the deadly use of poisons, of explosives, of guns, knives, swords and their bare hands."

Janine frowned. Mister Chang paused, respectfully. A few seconds passed while she contemplated, then she waved a hand for Mister Chang to continue.

"The Scottish Parliament were feeling vulnerable as they fended off approaches from King James to merge them with the English Parliament. The slogan of "One king, one parliament" was ironic for the Highlands of Scotland, as some regarded it as having not one, but two, potential monarchs. The idea of disposing of the Queen of the West and removing her as a problem was an enticing solution for the followers of King James. This put you and your mother in severe danger."

"My mother. The Queen," murmured Janine, almost to herself, as if testing the words on her tongue.

"As part of my advanced training in China," Mister Chang continued, "I studied with the monks of an ancient order at their monastery in the mountains. From them I learned the arts of mind control and, in particular, I learned a technique known in Europe as 'hypnosis'.

"With sufficiently intense exposure, over a long enough period, it is possible to change an individual's personality, their conduct, their beliefs and even their memories."

Mister Chang left his chair and approached Janine, prostrating himself face down on the cold stone tiled floor of the chamber.

"Your Majesty, I have made you other than you were," he said, his voice catching in his throat.

"How do you know that I am she?" Janine demanded, curtly.

Mister Chang looked up, utterly astonished.

"Your Majesty," Mister Chang protested, "I have trained you! My step daughter, Genji, who is a Fourth Level Master of the Martial Arts, has trained you. It is impossible that I could be mistaken. It is doubly impossible that both she *and* I could be mistaken."

Janine sat in silence for a full minute. Nobody in the room spoke. Mister Chang remained on the ground.

"Stand," Janine ordered, feeling it strange that she was quickly becoming comfortable with giving commands.

Mister Chang stood.

"Your Majesty," said Mister Chang, bowing low.

"Do not prove to me who I am," Janine said, "Prove it, instead, to everybody else in this room. Then I will be satisfied. If I am the one you say, then I may believe as you trained me to believe. They, however, will believe only what they see and what they hear."

"Very well, Your Majesty," Mister Chang said, bowing even lower.

Mister Chang motioned for everyone to stand and he led them to the centre of the chamber, leaving his stepdaughter by the fire.

"Genji!" He called.

Genji obediently leapt to her feet, a motion so graceful and elegant that she might have been a young deer or gazelle.

"Genji," Mister Chang commanded, "Kill the queen!"

CHAPTER 18

Having discounted the idea of simply shooting on a whim, Alex and Hamish returned to a more measured and reasoned consideration of their plight.

"I have a strange feeling about this," Hamish confessed.

"Yes, I know what you mean," Alex replied, "Is this real or have we both taken a heavy blow to the head, while ducking under a tree back there, perhaps?"

Hamish made the Scottish noise to show his grudging amusement.

"I have hold of a musket," Hamish said, "It has a trigger. It has a sparking drum. It has a powder pan. It has a full charge of powder in its breech. It has a lead ball ahead of the powder. It has a barrel. I am holding it and I am pointing it."

Alex said nothing, happy to let this jewel of observation hang in the air.

"Where do the mechanisms end?" Hamish mused, "With the trigger? Where the ball leaves the musket?"

He paused and was silent for several long seconds before continuing.

"Or are we, too, nothing more than pieces of machinery? At least to God? Or, maybe, to the power of nature? Or to the universe?"

Alex made a contemplative noise to indicate that he was pondering the proposition. After this, it was over a minute before anybody spoke and it was Hamish who broke the silence.

"Back in the times of the ancients, when Kiffan the Defiant fought against the Viking invaders, she was taken prisoner and was about to be put to death, when a tree burst into flames and burned for seven days and seven nights without damaging so much as a single leaf."

"I have heard the story," Alex confirmed, "Urokmort, who was the king of the Vikings, saw the tree aflame and spared her life for fear of angering the gods."

"And, since then, the presence of the almighty force behind this world has revealed itself in the form of a flame."

"To those it chooses to do its will," Alex added.

"I can't tell you how I know, but I absolutely know for certain, that when the time comes, we will know when to fire."

"When we were children," Alex whispered, "When we were hunting squirrels with our catapults, we would get a good aim for the shot, then – if one of us thought the moment had come to let loose – we would open our mouth, then clack our teeth together."

"A little less mysterious," Hamish grinned, "But every bit as useful."

CHAPTER 19

Inside the McCarthy stronghouse, Burberry peered down at the pistol that had been thrust under his chin. He was fascinated to see the gunpowder in the flash pan trickling away over the side as the steep angle of the barrel allowed gravity to work its mischief. Within a second, Burberry had made up his mind. This pistol was unlikely to fire and he was probably going to die, anyway, if he didn't do something quickly.

The McCarthy's lips were back against his ear and he inwardly shuddered at the mental image of his stinking mouth.

"Tell the person out there on that landing that you are in here. Tell them you have been tied up and abandoned," his captor snarled, "Say nothing else unless you want to die!"

Constable Burberry closed his eyes. He took in a deep breath. He firmed his resolve.

"He's in here!" Burberry yelled, rejecting his captor's script, and then added: "He has a pistol and a knife!"

The McCarthy jolted in shock and disbelief and made a bewildered gasp as his brain fought to accept what had just happened. Burberry, on the other hand, suffered no such confusion. Despite his arms and upper legs being tightly bound, he found that feet and his lower legs, below the knees, were still free to move. Lifting a foot and using all the force he could muster, Burberry worked it like a blacksmith's hammer, making three vicious stamps with the heel of his boot. The first stamp saw him gouge the sharp edge of his heel all the way down the front of the man's shin. The second, a moment later, saw the heel come down onto his victim's toes. The third saw his heel drive viciously into the man's instep.

The McCarthy howled with pain like a soul in torment. Burberry threw his head heavily to the left and, as he did so, he heard the unmistakable metallic whirr of the pistol's sparking drum rotating. The barrel dislodged from under Burberry's chin, skimming up his cheek and striking him painfully at the top of his eye socket. There was a bright flash as the sparse remnants of gunpowder popped weakly in the ignition pan, but – as he had hoped – it was insufficient to set off the charge.

CHAPTER 20

In a clump of trees across from the stronghouse, Alex and Hamish's mouths popped open, then shut, their teeth striking together loudly. Immediately, their Italian hunting muskets kicked in their grasp as smoke and yellow flames erupted from their muzzles.

CHAPTER 21

The McCarthy holding Burberry let out a venomous curse. His grip on the constable slipped. Burberry dropped his head, pushing his chin against his chest, just as there was a loud crash from the window.

Letting go of his pistol, the McCarthy's hand flew to his knife and he began to withdraw it from its sheath. Just then, two parallel blurred streaks of lead hurtled through the midst of the splintering glass panes. One ball hit the McCarthy's cheek, causing the side of his face – from his top lip to his temple – to shear away in a bloody mass. The second ball struck him in his throat, just below his jaw, going clean through both his windpipe and his spine.

The man's head had barely begun slump forwards when there was a jet of flame and a deafening bang from the doorway. The soldier, who was crouching there, had discharged his pistol. The opposite side of the McCarthy's head splattered all over the wall as a lead ball tore through it, from one side to the other.

The very real pain in Constable Burberry's knees, as they slammed into the floorboards, gave him reassurance that he was still alive. A second later, there was a sickening thud as his left temple struck the butt of the McCarthy's pistol, where it lay on the floor. Within a second, he had blacked out. Behind him, the lifeless body of Stewart McCarthy tumbled to the ground. The knife he had been holding fell from his dead hand, clattered onto the stone hearth, and spun wildly in a circle before coming to a halt.

CHAPTER 22

Alex and Hamish ran back to the stronghouse and were gasping for breath as they arrived. The front door of the building had finally been smashed open and Hamish led Alex round to it.

The whiff of burnt gunpowder and torched hay was offensive and hung in the air along with a pall of bluish-grey smoke that drifted lazily out through the door to greet them.

The two attracted scant attention – bar a few sullen scowls – and were not accosted by anyone. The soldiers, who were busily absorbed in individual tasks, grudgingly ignored the civilian trespassers in their midst.

At the top of the steps, through the gloom, appeared a pair of soldiers. They were supporting a third person, between them. The soldiers were clearly struggling to accommodate their number across the width of the stairs. The man they supported was dazed and finding it hard to walk. After grappling with him for a little while, one of the soldiers came to the front to hold his legs and the other grabbed him under his arms from the rear. In this fashion, they were able to lumber their way down to the hall below.

When, triumphantly, the little group reached the door, the man who had been carried lifted his head. Despite his face being dirty, spattered with blood and having a swollen lump over one eye, neither Hamish nor Alex had any trouble in identifying the features as being those of Constable Burberry.

"I'm glad it's you," Hamish announced, in mock surprise, "Because Caitlan was wondering if you wanted a couple of eggs with your breakfast. You weren't in your room, so we decided to track you down to ask you."

Burberry made a reasonable attempt at a laugh and then settled for awkwardly shrugging his shoulders.

"I have a fierce hunger on me," Burberry advised, apologetically, "You don't suppose she could stretch that to three eggs, do you?"

"Hark! You're one greedy haystack of a man!" Hamish exclaimed, "I suppose she can manage that, at a push, but you may be hearing complaints from the hens!"

They all began to chortle and snigger, but Burberry grimaced from the pain it caused him in his ribs. As the soldiers hauled him to his feet, he looked down at himself with disdain.

"If you'll excuse me, gentlemen, I need to wash for breakfast," he declared, "I seem to have got dirt under my fingernails."

In response to Burberry's attempts to stagger, the two soldiers – who had installed themselves either side of him – helped him forward into the welcoming hug of his two loyal friends.

After what felt like a long while, the three of them straightened up, taking their heads from each other's shoulders, and exchanged the kind of angst-laden look that men give each other when they know that words are completely ineffective. Women, in this situation, would have flung themselves back into an even more strenuous hug, but these were men. As such, they shared a code of behaviour governing physical contact and they knew that they were at its boundary.

"You're in trouble, anyway," Alex advised the constable.

Burberry looked around, feigning confusion. Alex leaned close, as if confiding a secret.

"You left your blankets in a mess when you got out of bed, this morning!"

Burberry guffawed and then suddenly cried out, wincing in pain.

"Stop! That hurts!" He begged, gripping his sides and groaning.

"We can provide you with a wagon, Sir, if it would assist you?" A sergeant offered.

"I think that would be an excellent idea!" Replied Burberry.

With a minimum of fuss, the army mustered a pair of fine black-and-tan horses and a flatbed wagon with a canvas cover that could be hoisted over a set of hoops. Their sparse belongings, including pistols, muskets, bows and quivers, were loaded into the back. Next, they stacked several sacks of grain and added a liberal amount of hay.

The constable, once he had been made comfortable on this rudimentary bed, insisted on taking a hold of his beloved gun and inspecting it before he would allow them to move off. Alex and Hamish waited, reverently, until the inspection was complete and the weapon duly stowed.

Although Alex drove the wagon slowly and carefully to spare Burberry as much buffeting as possible, it was a losing battle. The wagon rocked and swayed, sliding into ruts and bouncing over potholes. Presently, the track became slightly less challenging and they were able to speed up.

"I have cause to thank your stable lad," Burberry announced, abruptly.

"For what reason?" Asked Hamish.

"I told him that if I were unduly delayed that he should take himself off to where my escorting soldiers were camped and alert them."

Hamish's head whipped round and he opened his mouth to speak, but Burberry cut him off with the answer to his question.

"I told the lad that if he breathed a word to anybody, most especially you, I would tie him up by his thumbs and his big toes, smother him in honey, and hang him from a tree next to a wasp nest, then rattle and poke it with a stick!"

"He still should have said something," protested Hamish.

"Not after I told him that they would sting him ten thousand times and then crawl into his head through his nose and lay eggs in his brains!"

"And would they?" Alex asked, in a comical voice.

"Only if they were Campbell wasps!" Hamish retorted.

They all laughed and Burberry hugged his sides, grimacing in pain and gritting his teeth as he hissed through them.

Before long, they reached the point where Hamish and Alex had tied up their horses earlier in the day. Untying them from the tree, Hamish duly tethered the two animals to the rear of the wagon, where they trotted along contentedly behind it.

Hamish pointed to the missing thumb nail on the constable's hand.

"You left a part of you in the snow," he said, "And, by some miracle, we spotted it."

Burberry grunted.

The wagon reached the junction with the main road and, without the oppressive darkness of the forest, their mood began to lighten.

"If there had been only three of those men instead of four, I could have taken them!" Burberry boasted, puckering his lips to indicate frivolity.

"I dare say you're right!" Hamish responded.

Constable Burberry, lost in his thoughts, said nothing further from his infirmary in the back of the wagon, and his two companions did not press him. After a little way down the road – only marginally less strewn with ruts and holes than the previous leg of their journey – the big man relented.

"This reminds me of the times when, as a lad, I would run away from home and, on my return – having always got into some kind of trouble or mischief – I had to explain myself to my father and submit myself to a strapping."

Hamish scoffed at this remark, "We'll only give you the strapping if we think you deserve it."

"Ouch! Ouch! Ouch!" Cried Burberry, again clutching his sides as he laughed, "Don't jest! It hurts my ribs!"

"Who says we're jesting?" Alex challenged, "We might just take your britches down right now!"

"Stop! Please! Don't make me laugh!" Burberry begged, "Why is everything so damned funny to people in these parts?"

"Just about every day, in the Highlands, is cold, wet and miserable," Hamish explained, "We learn to ignore the cold. We learn to live with the wet. We learn to dilute our misery with any opportunity for laughter we can get."

"Aye, it's true!" Alex agreed, "I've always found it that way."

Hamish snorted in derision, indicating that Alex might not be a true Highlander.

"I may be a 'Southerner' from Dunfermline…." Alex pointed out, "But I'm only a good stone's throw away from the **real** Scotland!"

Burberry yelped in pain, as he joined in their laughter, and then gave a long, agonised groan.

"What have I told you?" He demanded.

Hamish and Alex chuckled and this brought yet more groans of pain from their passenger.

After a little while they stopped and helped Burberry off his back and into a sitting position in the nearest corner of the wagon. Resting himself against the sides of the wagon, he ran a supporting arm along the top edge, left and right. There he sat, grim faced, while Alex and Hamish rocked themselves enthusiastically from side to side to sway the vehicle. Evaluating the relative comfort of his new posture, Burberry declared it superior to the agony of lying down flat.

Alex returned to the driver's bench and the wagon rumbled off, again. Despite his continuing best efforts, Alex could not avoid them being bounced over the uneven road surface.

"I feel like an acorn in a beer barrel!" Burberry complained.

Alex slowed down a little more and plotted his course with even greater care.

"I'm sorry, but there aren't so many as five paces without a hole or a rut!" Alex apologised.

Hamish pushed some empty corn sacks down between the constable and the sides of the wagon and tucked some hay into the gap at the bottom of his back. The patient grunted his gratitude and gripped the sides of the vehicle even tighter.

Alex gave the horse a command in Gaelic and it completely ignored him.

"Slow there!" Hamish urged.

The horse obligingly adopted something approaching a funeral pace.

"So, the horses in the Scottish armies speak English?" Alex mused with a broad smile on his face.

"Yes, just like King James!" Hamish whispered, making his words hushed.

Alex put a finger to his lips and comically shushed Hamish, very noisily.

"Don't wake our passenger!" He cautioned.

Burberry almost exploded with indignation.

"Wake me? Do you think it possible that **anybody** could **ever** doze off in the back of this thing?" He demanded, "You'd need to hit them over the head with something!"

Burberry raised a hand, defensively, as his friends both turned to consider the merits of the proposal.

"I was whispering," Hamish confided, "To avoid the risk of you injuring yourself, internally, in response to my needle-sharp wit."

The constable made a groaning noise and arched his back as he fought to contain his amusement. They travelled for a full ten minutes before there was any further conversation.

"At the risk of you giving me that strapping," the constable began, gruffly, "I have to confess my stupidity to you both and what I did, today."

CHAPTER 23

Alex and Hamish in the front of the wagon, turned and cast Ewan Burberry, in the back, a caustic glance.

"My misfortune, today, was because I sneaked away on my own," Burberry admitted, "I ventured across the fields and up around the back of the McCarthy land. I took myself along the ridge behind the forest. I was interested in assessing the lay of the land. I was curious, too, about the McCarthy defences and how well they might patrol the edge of their territory."

"And?" Hamish asked.

"And I took the butt of a musket across the back of my head for my trouble. I had made my way down the bank and was following a thin trail into the trees. There were no trip wires or bell lines to be seen. I must have convinced myself that I had little to worry about, as I was creeping along as if stalking a deer."

"But?" Hamish and Alex chorused, together.

"But I was wrong. I reached the little clearing, where you found my thumbnail, and I was taken by surprise. I heard the musket being swung, with a swish in the air, but I did not have time to dodge it. There were three of them and they jumped me good and hard. Unfortunately for them, the blow to my head actually threw me into a rage."

"Go on," invited Hamish.

"My wrath was well and truly roused! It's strange to consider what shame and annoyance can do to a person. It made me see red! I punched them, kicked them, and threw them over and did my best to trample on them, but they were strong and handled themselves like they were used to brawling."

"I'm guessing that more than a few losing hands of cards end up in a fight when men of that kind are playing!" Hamish suggested.

"They are thugs!" Alex sneered, "No better than pigs or vermin!"

"I know plenty of pigs and vermin that look very much like royal courtiers when compared to them!" Replied Burberry, pretending to be offended on their behalf.

"So," Hamish announced, "You thought you would go and pay the McCarthys a visit, not with a band of armed troops, but all by yourself?"

Burberry shook his head and glowered.

"It wasn't the best decision of my life," he confessed, "And not one that I will look back on with pride!"

Alex and Hamish exchanged smirks and Burberry cursed them and began grinding his teeth.

"They beat me far beyond anything reasonable and then marched me up to their stronghouse," Burberry explained, "And, there, they threatened me with branding, castrating, blinding and scalding with oil."

"Always the impeccable hosts!" Hamish laughed.

"They were not happy that I had killed one of their number, the previous day. They were looking for vengeance. They are, to be sure, not the nicest of people, but – for McCarthys – they restrained themselves pretty well."

Hamish and Alex spontaneously sniggered, loudly, in mockery.

"I was sure that they would stretch my neck with a rope or, at the very least, take off a hand, but – despite their threats – they appeared resigned to just vigorously beating me and no more."

"That is strange," Hamish replied, "To hold back like that, they must have been acting under orders and those orders must have come from someone they feared."

"From what I gather," said Alex, "The McCarthys neither fear nor respect much at all in this world!"

"Aye," Hamish agreed, "All they respect is brute force and naked power."

"Which compels us to ask," Burberry responded, "Who has the power to make a bunch of vile filth like the McCarthys do exactly what they want and nothing more?"

Without hesitation, Hamish and Alex replied in unison.

"The Campbell of Argyll!"

The constable nodded and asked the question they were all thinking.

"Why would The Laird Campbell not want me killed?"

"Whatever the reason," Hamish offered, "There would have to be something in it for him. He wouldn't do anything without some kind of reward!"

"Or," Alex ventured, "The Campbell fears the wrath of somebody else, far more powerful than he."

"I would hope," retorted Hamish, with genuine foreboding, "That we are not talking about The Duke of Cumberland."

"It is sad to say," Burberry advised, "That while the governments of Scotland and England are at odds with each other, The Duke of Cumberland misses no opportunity to ingratiate himself and elevate his status by doing the dirty work of King James."

Hamish turned to face the constable.

"**You** are the king's representative," he insisted.

"Aye," Burberry conceded, "But my role and my duties may not attract equal enthusiasm both sides of the border."

Hamish opened his mouth to speak, but was unable to find the right words and Burberry spoke what was on his mind, for him.

"As you will very well know, by now," he said, "I am for the queen."

"Does the King know that?" Hamish asked.

"The king knows whatever it suits him to know."

"Does the Duke of Cumberland know that you support the queen?"

"If he does, then he is either unconcerned about it or he sees it as an advantage in his plans."

Alex told the horses, in English, to stop and the wagon jarred to a halt.

"The problem," Alex announced, "Is this: Why would the King or Cumberland allow you to be beaten and abused but stop at having you killed?"

Hamish threw a hand to his mouth with such force that both of his companions heard the loud smack as it landed.

"We forgot to mention!" Hamish gasped, inclining his head to the side and looking pointedly at Alex, "We have met somebody who **did** want to kill you!"

Alex suddenly slapped a hand over his own mouth.

"Oh! Lord bless me! I forgot about that!" Said Alex, suddenly recalling the dramatic occurrences of the previous day.

"Forgot about what?" The constable demanded.

"This is something that one of us should have mentioned already," Hamish apologised, "In fact, a **long** time before now!"

Burberry held up his hands in exasperation and gave them a look of furious impatience.

"Yesterday," Hamish explained, "While you were away, we had a visit at the inn, from three extremely nasty and unpleasant characters."

Burberry looked at him in bafflement.

"They were seriously dangerous people," Hamish continued, "And they were looking for **you**."

The constable's face betrayed intense curiosity.

"They claimed to be former army acquaintances of yours. I was certain, from their description, that it was you they wanted to find. They did not detail their business, but I denied all knowledge of you."

"Where are they now?" Burberry asked.

"They are resting," Alex offered, trying to suppress a grin.

"Resting?" Asked Burberry, his face puzzled.

"Yes. Until Judgement Day," Alex snorted.

"We served them whisky," Hamish told him, "Then we served them eternal darkness."

Burberry nodded and looked thoughtful. After a moment, Hamish lifted a hand to face height and raised his index finger to draw attention. He waited until he had it before he spoke.

"There is still one question that remains unanswered and, I should think, might have a bearing on all these matters!"

The other two looked blank.

"What is the reason for you going to Inverness, Constable Burberry," Hamish enquired, "If I may ask you so directly?"

Constable Burberry glanced back and forth between Hamish and Alex a couple of times. He looked like a man with a secret. He looked like a man who would dearly like to share his secret, but who was unsure if he dared. Burberry scratched his chin, thoughtfully, but said nothing. In the end, it was Hamish who spoke up.

"You said you were on the king's business."

"Yes. That is right. I am," Ewan Burberry confirmed, sounding a little distracted.

A few moments passed before he spoke, again, absentmindedly.

"Or, at least, I **thought** I was."

CHAPTER 24

Annis quickly recognised their vulnerability and called for everyone to pull back. The riders promptly disengaged and rode their mounts to what appeared to be the safety of the yet untrampled grasses. Almost immediately, however, one of their horses was struck in its haunches by a spear.

Balgair, seeing the enemy archers making their way to the front line, gave the order to withdraw completely. This action was met by jeering and bawdy insults from their enemy. Beyond the injury of their pride, the riders got away without further incident and were clear of danger before the archers had time to loose off any arrows.

The captain of the Campbell reinforcements now made what was to prove a catastrophic mistake. Unwisely, allowing urgency to drive him, his error would cost his men their part in the battle. He marched his troops to the upper edge of the slippery mud and ordered them to circle across and around to approach the unprotected flank of the MacDonalds.

It was as they passed the halfway point, with the muddy stretches a short distance downhill of them, that the main McRory cavalry arrived on the scene. Unlike the foot soldiers, who had forced their way through dense trees and brambles at the top end of the gulley, the horsemen had been compelled to go the long way round. Their route across the narrow ridge, on the far side of the hill, bordered a treacherous drop so precarious that they had very nearly lost one of their horses over the edge.

Seeing the situation, they wasted no time in charging into an attack. The horses were glad to be back on land that didn't shift beneath them and were eager and willing to commit themselves to a full gallop down the gentle slope.

With their ears back and nostrils flaring, they thundered towards the enemy force with gusto.

The Campbells in their path froze on the spot, the recent encounter with McRory horses still fresh in the memory of their survivors. Ahead and to the right of them was the main part of the battle, with MacDonalds head to head with the Campbells. To their right, downhill, was a huge expanse of mud. Directly between the two were Annis and her Honour Guard, their highly polished armour and full helmets flashing in the golden beams of the sun.

The Campbell soldiers at the front of the newly arriving column came to a halt and began to clumsily file back the way they had come. In response to the furiously yelled commands of their officers, they stopped. They were now summoned to go forwards, at a run, and to rush the main body of MacDonalds. They all knew, full well, that the moment they advanced, Annis and her smaller contingent of horsemen would promptly charge them from the side. Meanwhile, the twenty-six strong principal McRory cavalry were already bearing down on them like a tempest!

The McRory bowmen, while everybody else had been occupied, had scuttled up the length of the gulley floor, climbed up the steep side and were now positioned in the bushes along its edge.

Without warning, their arrows began to clatter and thud into the Campbell reinforcements. The specially tipped arrows spun on contact with armour and drove holes into it or pierced human flesh all the way from front to back, depending on the fortune of the victim.

A second wave of the special arrows, shot even higher, took a heavier toll, this time managing to pierce all the way through the majority of armour.

Within moments, a third salvo came into them, these fired lower and closer to the ground to take them from the side as they lifted their shields to protect themselves from the arrows above.

With perfect timing, three seconds after the last arrow sank home, the main McRory cavalry burst into their formation, head-on, ripping through them as a pack of wild dogs might run into a flock of sheep.

There was loud metallic clanking as the horses' armour rang off swords, helmets and shields while their riders sliced and hacked at their adversaries from the saddle.

The cavalrymen then veered their horses to the right, avoiding the sea of mud, and galloped into the gaggle of Campbell archers who had been summoned to the fore, throwing them in all directions.

A group of MacDonald troops now came running down the slope in a full throated Highland charge. The large cohort of new Campbells, having already become increasingly disordered, now degenerated into a state of total confusion. A number of them, who had dashed away down the hill, had skidded in the mud and were now strewn on the ground. As they struggled to gain their feet, the McRory archers, who had raced after them to get within range, picked them off with deadly precision.

Further up the field, more Campbells blundered into the mud, fleeing the hooves of the cavalry horses and the long reach of their riders' swords. Before long, the McRory horsemen had begun deliberately shunting and herding their victims into the increasingly treacherous lake of mud and filth.

The McRory archers, returning to the main fray, began firing into the enemy as they slipped and slid while attempting to climb over their dead or dying clansmen. The thin rain that had started half-heartedly, was now getting heavier and a panic began to run through them.

The rearmost section of the reinforcements, still trudging their way up the gradient, could now see the carnage ahead of them. Suddenly, a large group of them turned tail and began to run back down the hill.

The McRory cavalry fanned out, going wide and clear of the Campbell's flank, and then rode back around at them, regrouping into formation as they came. The riders ploughed into the middle of the marching column, cutting them off from those at the head and those at the rear. The riders slashed into their ranks with their claymores, hacking down soldiers, left and right, and riding over them.

A number of the enemy, unwilling to take their chances in the mud bath, tried to go beyond the McRory cavalry, but then ran into a wall of advancing MacDonald warriors on foot.

The remaining Campbells now attempted to go around the bottom edge of the mud, but the horses had now churned up such a large area that firm ground was fast disappearing. As they struggled to find a path, they were greeted by Annis and her riders who had moved to intercept them.

The line of arriving Campbell troops came to a complete halt. Having already seen two clusters of their fellows flee, they seemed to have lost their appetite for battle and began to head back downhill to safety. The McRory cavalry allowed them to go, unhindered, and rode back across to the main battle zone. Half of those newly arrived MacDonalds were sent to join them.

The Campbell troops were now in disarray. Their reinforcements had lost their push to join up with their main force. The main bulk of the Campbells were now under attack front and rear by MacDonald infantry and on their flank by MacDonald cavalry.

The rain grew heavier and began to form tiny rivulets down the meadow. These ran pale red with the diluted blood from the dead bodies that were now piling up. Both footprints and hoof prints began filling with swirls of this red trickle and it made a macabre backdrop to the continuing slaughter. It was as if the grass, itself, were bleeding.

The MacDonald captains, who had deliberately allowed the Campbell forces to breach their front line at several points, formed their troops up into a solid line to push their foes to the edge of the gulley. The MacDonald soldiers used their pikes to link up their shields into a wall. The McRory horsemen took up positions behind them and used their horses to barge and shove the shield wall forwards, heaving the Campbells backwards and toppling them down into the gulley.

With a third of the new Campbell troops having deserted and a third of them strewn dead on the ground, the remaining members of their party were clearly dispirited. They had made repeated forays to join up as a main fighting group, but these attempts had been thwarted.

The new MacDonald troops were still energetic and motivated and their ferocity was beginning to wear down their opponents. The air was ringing to the sound of clashing swords and shields and to the cries of the combatants.

Balgair shook Gavin's arm to attract his attention and motioned to a line of troops coming up along the bank of the stream from the direction of the Spey. For a moment, both men were in a state of anxiety as they pondered the identity of this force. A few moments later, they both cheered as they spotted some of the Grant banners beginning to appear amongst them.

It wasn't long before the Campbells were aware of the size of their losses, both in terms of deaths and of deserters. To make matters worse, they were able to see the growing volume of Grant soldiers who were starting to arrive. At the foot of the meadow, the Grants were already attacking the stragglers of the Campbell runaways.

As if the Campbells were not already sufficiently under pressure, fate chose that very moment to unleash its full and terrible vengeance.

Suddenly, there was a roaring, bellowing and howling from the top of the hill. The hearts of the Campbell captains fell into their boots as the MacDonald reserve force, that had been camped an hour's march beyond the mountain, burst out of the woods. They came as a tidal wave of wrath, fury and rage, running and bounding down the slope, waving claymores, axes, spears and clubs as they came.

CHAPTER 25

The Campbell pipes began to screech the order to retreat and regroup. Hearing this, Queen Annis shouted to her guard to go forward with her and strike at the cluster of Campbell officers. Despite being separated from the main group of McRory cavalry, Annis exhorted her guards to press ahead. Balgair watched in horror as she thrust and cut her way into the Campbell throng, her Honour Guard struggling to reach her.

Balgair put his whistle to his mouth and blew long and hard, his ears popping with the exertion. The McRory horses, distributed across the field in small groups, responding almost as if they were puppets on invisible strings, each immediately scrabbled and skidded to a halt. Moving as one, filled with a primitive urgency and desperation, they came ramming and shoving their way through the swirling mass of the enemy.

Annis cut down, hard, with her riding sword against the blade of a smaller Campbell sword, glancing down its length. Cleaving through the hand guard, her blade sliced into the arm of the person wielding it. Moving with only two of her Honour Guards about her, Balgair saw her dangerously exposed. Another two of her Honour Guard now struggled to reach her, only ten strides away, kicking and cutting like men possessed to make the distance. Balgair spurred his horse on and managed to get directly behind Annis and pushed hard to try to get alongside her.

Annis parried a blow from another sword and kicked its owner square in the face. She slashed to cut into the shaft of a pikestaff that was being raised at her. As her blade made contact, it was struck hard by an axe swinging up to meet it. Her sword jarred in her hand and she felt the impact all the way up her arm. As quick as a flash, before the tremor had even finished, the axe was twisted, turning her sword in her hand and loosening her grip on it. Her heart missed a beat, then thudded with shock, as – with a skilful movement – the owner of the axe caught her weapon between the edge of its blade and one of the curved flat prongs that arched out from its end. With a sharp twist, she was disarmed.

She cursed herself! She should have predicted that move! Had this been single combat, she would have never fallen for such a trap. In the midst of battle, tired and weary, she had been clumsy. She had not been prepared for such unexpected mastery, coming out of the blue, like this!

Annis twisted in her saddle and brought her foot back, ready to yank it out of the stirrup, but it was already too late. She drove down her right arm, while raising her fist and turning it frontward, desperately attempting to deploy the small round shield she wore over her elbow. While this was a useful device for protecting her face or neck, under the right circumstances, she could not get it down low enough, in time, and her opponent's axe blade came up, underneath it, and cut deep into her underarm.

Annis screamed in pain and she felt blood begin to gush from the gaping wound. She looked down and, glimpsing the face of her attacker, she was incensed to see a crooked smile on his lips and a glint of satisfaction in his eye. This expression, however, changed instantly to one of consternation the moment he heard her cry. This was a female voice and the only possible female who would be on the battlefield would be his enemy's queen! This, they realised, was the famous girl warrior!

The Campbell fighter was shocked to recall the sheer force of the blow Annis had delivered. With terrifying clarity, his mind registered the dire nature of his situation! He spotted the gleaming bronzed helmets of four exceptionally capable personal guards around her. With a sickening thud, a stout club struck the side of his own helmet, knocking him off his feet. Next, not one, but two, mounted guards leapt from their horses, taking him to the ground. Like a wave of destruction, the other Honour Guards swept over and around him, flattening his comrades to either side of him like so many skittles and throwing others aside as if sweeping with a gigantic invisible broom.

Swaying uncertainly in her saddle, Annis was at the centre of a whirlwind of flashing, swishing, ringing steel. With some effort, she regained control of her horse, but then felt it being tugged and spun around. Slumping forward, she grabbed weakly at the neck of her horse. Pandemonium had broken out around her. Gavin had hold of her reins and was desperately guiding her horse out of the fray. Staring, wide eyed in total disbelief, her Honour Guard had been momentarily numbed with shock. The inconceivable had happened! A violation of their very purpose and existence. With herculean strength, her escort smashed and mangled every enemy soldier within reach. They swung. They gouged. They thrusted. They shouted and bellowed, venting their anger.

Like some strange and inexplicable telepathy, the news that Annis had been gravely injured flew around the battlefield like a bolt of lightning and its effect was overwhelming. The very air pulsed and crackled with a frenzied madness. The MacDonald troops tore into the Campbells with an almost superhuman fury. They seemed hardly able to suppress their boiling anger.

The original ranks of MacDonalds, who were part of the conflict from the beginning of the Campbell attack, believed that they were to blame. They feared that they should have fought harder and more fervently from the outset and that, as a result, they had failed her.

The Grants, now arriving from the foot of the hill, having come up the bank of the stream, felt that they had missed an opportunity to shine and show their worth in their new allegiance. Despite having already fought a pitched battle with the enemy for over an hour, they held themselves accountable for not arriving there sooner.

As the sky darkened and rain clouds began to roll and rumble above them, it became evident that none of the allies were merely fighting the Campbells, anymore. Each of them were fighting their troubled conscience and their inner demons, too. The effect was astonishing! They swept like a tidal wave of vengeance through the Campbells. The Campbells could be forgiven for assuming that Satan, in person, had joined the fray!

CHAPTER 26

Wild Flower, of Clan Grant, sat in the branches of a tree at the highest point of the gulley. She knew that Annis had been wounded, but knew for sure that, if treated soon, it would not be fatal.

Wild Flower smiled a sad but knowing smile. She knew that the soldiers were inflamed by the powerful spirits that lived in their blood. In her learnings from the ancient ones, Wild Flower used the Gaelic words for the secret spirits of the blood.

She called the one 'sguabadh spiorad' or "shock spark". This spirit appeared in response to surprise or fear and allowed an individual to respond vigorously and energetically.

She called the other 'gaisgeach connadh' or "hero fuel". This boosted a person's strength, increased their endurance and made them many times more daring.

She knew that, one day, these special things would be called 'adrenaline' and 'testosterone', but she was happy to call them 'blood spirits' for those were names appropriate for the time and age.

Abruptly, she felt something calling to her. She opened her mind and felt the presence of the eagle from the mountains. It was telling her something. It was telling her that there was danger. She felt it, rather than saw it, as the bird leapt off the cliff edge and took to the air. She knew that it was coming. She could hear the dull roar of the wind whistling past its head. She could feel the thrill of its dive. She knew that its huge wings were tucked back. She could feel its urgency.

There was something wrong. There was something she could not see. There was an event that evaded her.

Something was about to happen, but it was hidden from her. She struggled to see what was about to happen, but could not.

She felt a sense of panic. Was this not her time? Was this not her moment? She reached out to the bird. She sensed its commitment and resolve. This was not her time. This was not her moment. This was the bird's time. This was the bird's moment. She felt its certainty.

'What,' she wondered, struggling for inspiration, *'Could an eagle have to do with two armies waging war?'*

CHAPTER 27

Balgair ordered a close formation to assemble around him as he dragged Annis across onto his own horse and placed her at the front of his saddle. She was losing a lot of blood and he was extremely worried.

Her Honour Guard battered and bludgeoned their way through to safety and now, clear and in the open, they galloped with manic haste to the foot of the slope.

Their party crashed and clattered across the rocks at the bottom of the gulley and reached the opposite side. Balgair swung down from his horse, clutching Annis awkwardly, and Gavin grasped hold of her to help Balgair lower her to the ground. Sachairi appeared and began shouting commands. Immediately, cloaks and sheepskins were produced from all directions and Annis was nestled into them.

Wild Flower sprang from out of nowhere. She was holding a cotton bag of herbs and potions and carried a large clump of moss and several cotton wads.

"First, we need to stop the bleeding," Wild Flower announced, coolly and completely unflustered.

She removed the queen's helmet and set a rolled up blanket to support her head. She then busied herself tending to the queen's wound, moving quickly and expertly, all the while humming a strange little tune. Her patient stared blankly and with complete disinterest. Balgair and Gavin looked worried at her expression.

"Her mind is not alert," Wild Flower explained, "It is as though a bolt of lightning has struck her brain. She can no longer think or feel what is happening to her. Just like a rabbit runs and dives into its burrow when in peril, her mind has gone to safety and drawn away from her."

Wild Flower's words were so composed and her behaviour so unruffled that those around her rapidly calmed and the stench of their fear receded. She beckoned a young soldier to kneel by her and placed his hand over the queen's wound and showed him the right way to press down on the dressing. She commanded Gavin to remove his belt and quickly fastened it around Annis' arm and pulled it tight to stem the flow of blood. Next, she had several other soldiers undo their boots and sandals. They did so without hesitation. Wild Flower promptly commandeered their leather laces and used them to strap in place an improvised bandage she had applied.

Wild Flower undid the buckles and straps on the queen's upper body armour and, as gently as she could, slid off her chest plate, followed by her neck guard. Next, she unfastened her loin guard, her thigh plates and finally her shin shields. After this, she very carefully undid the fixings of the sculpted metal casing over her upper and lower arms.

Annis only wore metal plating to cover the outside of her arms. This was to reduce the weight she had to carry in combat. She had always shunned full arm protection because, she claimed, it reduced her agility. The vicious wound inflicted on her had been by a thrust up the soft, exposed underside of her arm.

Under Gavin's direction, the soldiers took blankets and sheets and lashed them together to fix a body sling between a pair of pike staffs. These were then suspended between two horses.

Beyond the gulley, the screams and cries of battle continued. A full scale slaughter was being delivered upon the Campbells. The smell of gunpowder was heavy in the air and random clouds of smoke drifted and billowed across the grass, forced this way and that by the changing wind.

The Grants had formed a protective line to shield the queen and her attendants. The earlier panic had now given way to some kind of order. The troops in this emergency retinue were now gathering things together in preparation to move off.

Wild Flower, though pressed to do so, would give no assurance as to how well Annis would heal and refused to say if she were likely to make a full recovery. She did, however, say that she had seen people survive and mend with worse injuries and that some of those had been where they had not received such timely treatment.

Balgair and Sachairi tested the sturdiness of the stretcher between the horses and carefully checked the lashings, pulling and tugging, until they were satisfied with their reliability. One of the young attendants was shocked to be picked up and thrown, forcefully, into the apparatus to test it. Everybody declared it fit for purpose.

Gavin, Balgair and Sachairi had been soldiers for their whole lives and this had developed in them the unusually heightened awareness that experience military men grew to possess. It was this strange sensation that kicked in, now, as they lifted Annis to sit upright between them in interlinked arms.

"Threat!" Gavin shouted, his body stiffening and his pulse racing.

The Grants, several paces forward of them, scrambled into a protective formation. The McRory fighters drew their weapons and those closest lofted their shields to draw around as a barrier.

There was a muffled grunt from behind a group of rocks at the edge of the gulley and a spear came hurtling out of the hazy smoke. The spear surged between two McRory shields before the gap could be fully closed. It was thrown exceptionally hard by a highly skilled spearman and it was aimed with deadly accuracy directly at Queen Annis, perfectly aligned to strike her cleanly in the heart.

Balgair saw it coming and a shock of abject terror ran through him as he drove his foot hard into the ground to turn himself. The next thing he knew, he was watching himself shift with amazing slowness as time began to slacken and decelerate. Everything appeared to move at a tenth of its normal pace. He stepped forward and then launched himself with all his might into a leap. The action unfolded with infuriating lethargy as he saw and felt every moment and every heartbeat.

Balgair realised that he could not make the distance to put himself in front of the spear. With gruelling effort, he tried to force his body to go faster, but nothing he did affected the sickeningly unhurried elapse of time.

As he looked at the queen his soul wrenched and heaved with unbearable agony. She was still unaware of her surroundings, looking detached and slightly confused. He suddenly realised that she was blinking and was surprised that he could actually see her eyelids very slowly coming down and then raising up again.

He saw Gavin, at the corner of his vision, his face conveying alarm and mounting terror. For some eerie reason, he knew, beyond doubt, that Gavin was seeing everything with the same slowness. The dawning realisation and crippling anguish on Gavin's face, as he watched, was utterly heart-breaking to witness!

All of a sudden, Balgair found he had tears in his eyes. He could feel them, hot and stinging. He could feel his chest shake with a spasm of grief. He knew that Gavin could see him. He knew that he could see him crying, but he did not care. He knew how his features must be twisted, but it mattered nothing to him.

Balgair became aware that his lips were moving and he knew that a sound was coming from them. He concentrated and focused his mind and suddenly knew that he was reciting The Lord's Prayer. Now in control of himself, he began to say the words with renewed passion and purpose.

In this excruciating torture of distorted time, his mind raced at a bewildering speed. He found himself telling God how sorry he was for all the things he had done in his life that were wrong and how he regretted the things he should have done that he hadn't. Most fervently of all, he told God how, if only He would let Queen Annis live, he would happily die a thousand times in the most fearsome pain and agony. He told Him that he would gladly go to Hell and suffer everlasting damnation and eternal misery if only He would spare her. He told his mother that he was sorry for running away to join the army and for leaving her and his little brother behind. He told her that he was sorry that he had broken her heart. He knew, now, for no explicable reason, how long she had mourned him and how many nights she had cried herself to sleep. He recalled how, in a dream, she had appeared to him and told him that she completely forgave him for any wrong he had done her. She had insisted that her presence would only ever be a prayer away if he ever needed it. Now he prayed to her, entreating her to join his own prayer and begging her to ask that Annis should be spared. He beseeched her to tell God that there was nothing – absolutely nothing – that he would not do in return for her life.

Balgair looked back to Gavin, wholly unashamed, and saw that the other was regarding the queen with a strange look in his eye. It was a look he could not place. Balgair looked to Annis, too, and was startled at what he saw.

The ring on her finger was lit with a yellow and orange glow. It pulsed and cascaded a fiery light that seemed to weave and cavort in the air. Suddenly it flashed a bright plume of flame that hovered and shimmered like a halo above it.

Balgair looked into the eyes of his queen and, in a fleeting moment, they lit with full awareness and understanding. She was back. She was with them. Her mind had finally returned. With a pang of regret, Balgair wished she were elsewhere, again, mindless of her imminent death. He wept inside. He cried out in his mind. He choked in anguish.

The spear was now only two paces from its target. With an absurd flash of consciousness that earned him his own instantaneous rebuke, he mentally congratulated the thrower of the spear on his aptitude and ability. He crushed the thought like snuffing out a candle.

Balgair was unaccountably aware that Annis had seen the spear. He couldn't say how he knew, but he knew it for certain. He also knew that she could be in no doubt and under no illusion what was about to happen to her. She was about to die. She was about to die and he, Balgair, was cursed to witness it, completely helpless to intervene.

She did not look away. She ignored the spear. She was, instead, holding her gaze on him. She smiled. She smiled the sweetest, most beautiful smile he had ever seen. He felt his heart shatter into a thousand tiny fragments.

Without shifting his eyes from those of Annis, for some mystifying reason, Balgair could see Wild Flower, uncannily outside of his normal range of vision. She was smiling, too, but her smile was the wry and sardonic smile of someone who knew a secret that they were not about to share.

Wild Flower was aware of him. Balgair could tell it. She spoke to him inside his head.

'You are a good man. A man who is worthy of asking for a miracle,' she said with complete calmness.

His mind was unable to process this statement, so he pushed it to one side in his head.

'That,' she added, *'Is why it was necessary for **you** to be here.'*

Balgair was outraged!

'What?' Balgair shouted in his brain, *'It was necessary for me to watch this heroic woman as she dies?'*

Wild Flower was looking up. Her gaze was fixed on something just above them. Balgair could not force his eyes to move. He wondered if he should return to his prayers, but – for some peculiar reason – he knew that they were no longer needed.

Those present that day would all be adamant about the noise that followed. They would be willing to solemnly swear as to the accuracy of their memory. They would testify that – at that precise moment – there was a colossal clap of thunder. Balgair didn't hear it. He heard a voice, instead. The voice was deep and kind and overpoweringly good. The voice said three words:

'So be it.'

The words were in him. The words were around him. The words were booming in the clouds in the sky above him. The moment they were spoken, Balgair felt profoundly soothed and at peace.

He looked at Annis, Queen of the West, and he smiled back at her. Her eyes twinkled at him. She was happy. She was, now, at peace with these traumatic events. She was perfectly calm.

The spear was now only an arm's length from its target. In real time she would perish in a fraction of a second. The spear was almost upon her, but it was okay, now.

'What?' Balgair asked, in his head, *'How can it be okay?'*

He saw the blood. There was so much blood. He was taken aback by how much blood. He watched the blood as it shot into a little cloud. He saw it puff and blossom in a circular crimson wave. He saw it fill the air between them with a fine mist that blew hot and wet on his face. He saw it splash across Annis' face, too. It even drenched Wild Flower's features, her upturned face catching it full across her brow and her cheeks.

The blood was preceded, an instant before, by a flash of white. A flash of white and light grey, tipped with yellow. It was a streak so rapid that, even at **this** fantastic level of awareness, it was still a blur. It passed between them with such speed that it could have been a white cannon ball that had been fired from the sky.

CHAPTER 28

The spear that had been thrown at Annis stopped and abruptly changed direction. It did not reach her. The spear was struck with such force that it dropped downwards to the ground.

The spear had, draped around it, the sprawled and lifeless body of a magnificent and majestic eagle.

CHAPTER 29

Having been told to kill Janine, Genji did not hesitate. She approached like a mountain wildcat, stealthy and agile, moving to position herself within range to pounce.

Janine's mind spun and gyrated wildly. She blinked and screwed up her eyes in an effort to concentrate. How would her mysterious protector reach her, here? How could he possibly find her? She was completely defenceless and beyond his care! For once, she was alone!

Vaguely, in the distance, she began to hear the tinkling of tiny bells. Mister Chang was looking directly at her. He raised his hands, palms together as if in prayer, then – parting them at the very top – he tapped three times with the tips of his fingers.

It was as if the gesture had popped a bubble within Janine's head. It felt, to her, as though Mister Chang had physically reached into her mind. She had a sensation of being a jack-in-the-box that had leapt out from the cube that was its prison.

The nothingness that she had felt approaching – that empty void that always took her after the sound of the little bells – wavered for a second and then receded.

'I am here,' said a voice in her head.

The voice was unmistakable. It was her own. Janine blinked and slapped her hand to her forehead, as if she might be able to swat the voice like a fly on her brow.

The bells had come to take her, but they had relented. She seized the thought, as if capturing a scurrying mouse by its tail. This glimmer of insight that had shot past her was still within reach. She retrieved it, gripping it firmly, and dragged it back to her. She had, indeed, been drifting into a dull emptiness. It was the dreamless void that embraced her whenever her life was in danger. Now, however, it had been held back. She suddenly realised that whatever was about to happen was about to occur with her full awareness.

'*Be calm,*' the voice that was her own said and she became utterly relaxed.

Abruptly, at this moment, the whole world suddenly clicked into slow motion. Janine closed her eyes and concentrated, heedless and fearless of Genji's approach. Janine's mind sped through her train of thought with meteoric rapidity. Why was the dreamlike feeling her friend? Why did it exist? What was its purpose? She drilled down, examining, dissecting and scrutinising it until her brain shuddered with a cataclysmic realisation: Mister Chang had released her inner mind so that she could know her other self.

In the few seconds that had passed, Janine estimated that she had processed at least ten minutes of thinking. Her mind seemed to be capable of the most amazing feats of analysis! It was able to pose questions and then solve them almost instantaneously!

Her perception of her surroundings had become incredibly acute. With the briefest, most cursory glance, she could absorb even the tiniest detail. This new perception now seemed to be tapping her on her shoulder to draw her attention. She became overwhelmingly aware of another's presence. It was as if somebody had been standing in front of her but she had only just become alert to them. With bizarre and inexplicable insight, she realised that the other person was herself. She studied herself with total detachment. She was not two people – she decided – but, rather, two people were her.

CHAPTER 30

Genji would now need just two more steps to strike. Janine knew, intuitively, that she would only use one. The world was still moving at a bizarrely gradual pace. The excruciating slowness with which Genji sprang, she knew, was not real.

Janine turned to the side with blistering speed and brought up both of her hands. She held them close to her body, one higher and upright in front of her face, the other lower and horizontal with her palm downwards. No sooner had she adopted this stance, than Genji was upon her.

Janine leaned her head away as a foot cruised across in front of her face. The foot was followed by a fist. At her new level of consciousness, these ponderous actions seemed laborious and dawdling, but were actually a streaking blur. With calmness that baffled and astonished her, Janine took a step back and flipped to her left with the grace of a ballet dancer, striking Genji in her side.

Despite the blow, Genji tumbled nimbly through the air, with amazing agility, and landed on her feet. Fluidly diverting the force of her motion as she went, Genji spun around and lifted her foot impossibly high, aiming a kick at Janine's temple. As if the kick had been signalled in advance, Janine's counter kick swept it aside. Stepping quickly forward, Janine stretched to touch the ground with the fingertips of her right hand, while simultaneously lifting and curling back her left leg to strike Genji behind her ear. The glancing blow made Genji stumble for an instant before regaining her balance.

Genji's reply was prompt and, apparently, effortless. Her leg flew around in a long arc, knocking Janine off her feet. Janine used this new momentum to her advantage, harnessing it to roll into a handstand, then – with baffling ease – she sprang back to her feet.

As she straightened, Genji's next attack was already on its way. Her hand and foot punched and kicked, at the same time, as she made what seemed to be a tediously languid lunge. Janine blocked the move and tried to throw Genji off balance, but her opponent was already whirling to translate her thwarted move into another one.

Janine dropped to the floor, locked her feet around Genji's calves, then spun like a corkscrew with all her might. Genji began to topple, unable to recover from the unexpected manoeuvre.

At the table, witnessing this frantic and furious combat, The Duke of Bo'Ness turned in his seat, eager to follow the action, accidentally knocking a candlestick from the table. Janine watched it fall in a leisurely dawdle and knew the exact instant it would clunk against the stone floor. Genji mistook her glance for distraction and moved to exploit it. Janine was ready for her and, as the two of them leapt at each other, she was able to connect a blow while parrying that of her foe. They collided and both struggled to recover. Janine overstepped and Genji was able to strike again, immediately. Janine felt the impact on the side of her head and blinked in shock. She was only just able to suppress a gasp of pain.

Janine heard a sharp click and was shocked to see Genji flick open a knife that she had deftly slipped out from a concealed pocket. With a feeling of strangely detached horror, she realised that this girl did, indeed, intend to kill her!

The candlestick hit the floor and, with uncannily swift reflexes, Janine's hand shot out and caught it as it bounced, snatching it out of the air. With a jerk of her wrist, she upended the candlestick, nestling its narrow neck into the palm of her hand. Genji slashed with her knife, aiming across Janine's throat. Urging and exhorting the candlestick to move faster, Janine pushed as hard as she could, propelling it, with infuriating sloth, into the path of the knife. The impromptu weapon narrowly managed to intercept its target and rang with a satisfying 'ding!'.

Janine let go of the candlestick, still chiming, and allowed her hand to continue its course. Stretching out her fingers like an arrowhead, she jabbed Genji, hard, in the upper arm. Genji flinched but managed to twist and lift her elbow, sending it smashing into the side of Janine's jaw. As the elbow made contact, Janine whirled her head to the side, successfully avoiding most of the impact. With a lightning fast motion Janine swept her hand back to, first, slap the handle of the knife, then flipped it over to strike the inside of Genji's wrist. The knife fell from her grasp, tumbling and spinning towards the floor.

Janine drew her feet up from under her, as if leaping a hurdle, and let herself fall. In response, Genji reached and grabbed Janine's arm and attempted to push herself downwards, using her adversary for purchase. Janine flung off her hold and swung a kick, which she intentionally failed to connect. The motion rotated her out of Genji's range.

Descending with exquisite sluggishness, the two women landed at the exact same moment. Janine was already reaching for the knife, attempting to snatch it by the handle. Genji was clearly satisfied to simply remove it from the conflict and her hand was punching to knock it away. They both made contact with the knife at the same moment. Janine struggled to keep hold of it as Genji's blow threatened to dislodge it. After a desperate battle, the knife stayed between Janine's fingers but, in a flash, Genji's hand was flying up to reach for it.

Mister Chang got to his feet and folded his arms across his chest.

The knife was now held, tenuously, by both challengers. Scrambling to their knees, swinging left and right and wriggling like eels, the two attempted to throw each other over. Janine reached with her free hand and pulled Genji towards her, thrusting herself forward to deliver a head butt. Genji arched her back and tried to lift Janine off her knees to trip her. The knife, pointing upwards to the ceiling, ended up directly between them, in a shared grip, at throat level.

Genji and Janine fought to overpower each other, the knife swaying first one way and then the other. Their hands trembled with the effort and their faces grimaced with concentration. The blade teetered precariously between them, its tip glinting in the light.

"Stop!" Mister Chang shouted.

Instantly, the two women desisted. The knife fell to the floor with a clatter. Mister Chang clapped his hands and the two women stood and bowed reverently to each other.

"Your Majesty," said Mister Chang, "It is, now, no longer a mystery to you what exercises you were doing in the forest, with your mother, when you thought you were daydreaming."

CHAPTER 31

Janine turned to look at Mister Chang. He looked to the floor and bowed his head. Janine stared at him in complete astonishment. Gradually, her expression became one of dawning realisation. She had grown up living a lie. Everything about herself had been a lie. All she had learned and believed in, over the years, had been an elaborate deception.

She stood in a state of puzzlement, her mind racing. She was a servant. She was a lady's maid. That was the life she remembered. It was a perfectly ordinary, completely drab and dull existence. Now, it emerged, she was also a queen. A young woman of great significance whose life was in danger from powerful enemies.

She decided that she wasn't so much living a falsehood as living a life where only half of everything were true. She had a thousand questions she wanted to ask and, no doubt, for each one of them that was answered, she would have several more to follow.

She strained her mind to recall her past from as far back as she could manage. Her first memories were of being sat on a mat under a table, with chairs drawn close around to keep her from crawling out, and her mother working nearby.

She recalled her mother singing or humming most of the time and, when she wasn't doing either, she would be talking to Janine, telling her stories or reciting poems.

She recalled that their house was of a fair size for people of humble means. There had been four rooms, whereas most people made do with one or maybe two. Her mother did the cooking, washing and mending for better off families in the village. Sometimes she made dresses for the women and, now and again, even formal jackets and kilts for the men. She also turned her hand to spinning and weaving. She worked from first light in the morning until dusk, every day, from Monday to Saturday and from Lunch Time until dusk on a Sunday. On a Sunday morning she would go to the church, twice, once at daybreak and then, later, at mid-morning.

No matter how short of time her mother might be or how challenging her workload, she would always be available to help Janine exercise and keep fit. She would always set aside time for her to practise the art of deep thought in the woods.

Janine clenched her jaw, shut her eyes tightly and knotted her brows as she tried to recall her childhood experiences. An image swam from the back of her mind. She remembered having a sister when she was very tiny. Could this be true? Had there been a sister? No! Surely not! She had asked her mother and father about it, many times, but they had always laughed. They told her that they were certain they would not forget about a second child if there had been one! The recollection, be it false or not, gave her a pang of sadness and she felt a sensation of her heart being squeezed by an invisible hand. Her parents had always teased her when she asked about a sister. They told her that she must have been experiencing really vivid dreams.

Mister Chang waited patiently, allowing Janine time to absorb her situation, and held his tongue until he felt she had reached some kind of broad comprehension. He told himself that she needed to arrive at an understanding of her plight, no matter how much it filled her with bitterness and resentment. Only then would she be able to move forward.

Mister Chang watched Janine carefully as she continued to look deep in thought. Eventually, after she had displayed at least five different contemplative expressions in succession, she appeared to become calm and aware, again.

"Who are you?" Mister Chang shouted with sudden intensity, hoping to engage her years of study and training.

"I am a warrior. I am a queen," Janine replied, in mechanical recitation, "The two halves make my whole, for I am the one no more than I am the other."

"What must you do?"

"I must remain hidden. I must not allow myself to be discovered. I may defend myself when in danger, but only when my life is threatened."

"What is your line?"

"I am a Scot. I am a Pict. I am a Norse. I am from the blood of the first queen. I am a true born from the daughters of the line of Kiffan the Defiant."

"What do you hold dearest to your heart?"

"I have the petal of a violet," Janine replied, "I keep it in a glass thimble. I keep the thimble in a pouch. I keep the pouch in a box. It is my most precious thing because it is the symbol of my one true love."

Janine sank to her knees and, in unison, everybody else in the room dropped to their knees, as well.

"How can this be?" Janine asked, sobbing soundlessly, her shoulders heaving.

Mister Chang gave her an anguished smile.

"I have lived in darkness," Janine lamented, tears now streaming down her face, "I have lived hidden away! Hidden even from myself!"

Genji prostrated herself, face down, on the stone floor and she, too, began to weep.

Mister Chang was quiet and subdued. The act of confessing responsibility for most of the things that had caused Janine confusion, worry and distress had dented his appetite for talking.

Mister Chang had given her the "proof" she had demanded. He had demonstrated to her the combat skills that had secretly protected her. He had furnished her with the knowledge that she was, indeed, the Queen of the West. While the truth of it had been evident to everybody else in the room, it had only inflicted further upset on her.

"Your Majesty…" The Duke began, inclining his head.

"Please don't call me that!" Snapped Janine.

"But…" The Duke protested, patently flustered, "I am obliged to address you formally and with the title that befits you."

"I have been in hiding. I have been hidden away for half a lifetime. I am now only just aware of my full self. For all the life I knew I had been a nobody. I have, I promise you, been addressed far less politely than the title you propose. I have been addressed in ways that you can scarcely imagine! I have been beaten as a nobody, threatened as a nobody, starved and intimidated as a nobody," she scolded, "And leaping suddenly into blazing sunshine from darkness and gloom, to be addressed in **that** particular way distresses me!"

Her audience remained tight lipped and shuffled uncomfortably.

"Let us all agree," she said, "That I will, for the present, maintain the secrecy that I have known for so long and I will be addressed by the name familiar to me, which is 'Janine'."

The reaction to this proposal could be felt in the sudden change in atmosphere. There was no enthusiasm for it.

"For the purposes of your remaining unknown," The Duchess suggested with a bow, "It might be more in keeping if you were to at least be known as 'Your Ladyship', Your Maj...."

The Duchess stopped, abruptly, cutting herself short, and looked apologetic.

"Very well," Janine conceded with obvious distaste, "But only when you first speak to me, not over and over during a conversation."

"We are all most grateful," The Duchess replied and then added: "Your Ladyship."

Janine smiled indulgently and gave a little sigh.

"I have just survived a very energetic and determined attempt to kill me, defending myself using skills of which I was previously unaware!"

"You are no ordinary person," Mister Chang asserted, "And you have no ordinary future."

"I have no ordinary past!" Janine rebuked.

"We needed to keep you safe, Your Ladyship," The Duke implored, "And it was decided that the most effective option to hide you was to do so in plain and open sight."

"Just so," Mister Chang agreed, "For if there had been a guard constantly watching over you, it would have drawn attention. We needed to keep you safe. This is where training in the fighting arts was essential."

Janine looked at Mister Chang more sympathetically, "I suppose I did have a guard constantly watching over me?" She said, venturing an unenthusiastic smile.

"I trained you in combat using a variety of weapons that you might encounter, here in your country, and Genji trained you in the art of unarmed combat. She taught you in the way of *'The Iron Fist'*, which uses strength and power, and in the way of *'The Poisoned Hand'* which uses agility, stealth and suppleness."

At this, Genji rose, made a fist with one hand and pressed it against the flat, vertical palm of the other. Then she bowed to Janine, descending with fluid ease into a seemingly impossibly low stance. Janine closed her eyes for a brief second and then, with astonishing swiftness, dropped into the exact same pose. Genji beamed at her with unrestrained delight.

"You have trained me well!" Janine declared, now with a broad, warm smile illuminating her face.

"You were an amazing student!"

"You were a superb teacher!"

"You were **both** exemplary, Your Ladyship!" Mister Chang insisted.

Genji's faced dropped. She had forgotten Janine's status and the proper way to address her. Janine shook her head to dismiss the issue and maintained her amiable disposition.

"Do you remember the days of your training?" Genji asked, drawing the courage to ask a question.

"The memory swirls in my mind as I think of it. When I concentrate, the recollection slowly starts to come back to me. My heart beats faster at the recollection. I have an idea that I was very happy to learn!"

Genji smiled, undeniably pleased.

"I think you were surely my closest friend, Genji!"

Genji's smile suddenly faltered and failed. She looked awkward and − suddenly embarrassed − timidly fixed her eyes on her own feet. After a few moments, Genji shot a glance at Francesca, her distress increasing. Francesca stood quietly, a few paces away, her face ashen and her bottom lip beginning to tremble. She was unmistakably on the verge of tears. Janine's heart broke at the sight of her. She glanced back to Genji who returned her a pained, wistful smile.

"Francesca?" Janine called, her voice gentle.

Francesca looked up, her face crumpling with a misery she could scarcely contain.

"Francesca!" Janine said, "Please!"

Francesca's brow creased in puzzled and alarm at this choice of words.

"Francesca! You are my **other** closest friend!" Janine wooed, "Please, forgive a foolish, confused girl with no more wits in her head than a fruit fly!"

Francesca looked utterly forlorn but neither moved nor replied.

"Genji!" Commanded Janine, gesturing towards Francesca, "Kill my closest friend!"

Genji looked shocked, but swiftly adopted a fighting stance.

CHAPTER 32

"Genji!" Said Janine, modifying her previous order, "Kill her with love!"

Genji's troubled face lit up. She and Janine surged nimbly forward, simultaneously, and they swept Francesca into their arms. Within a moment, all three of them were hugging and crying.

The Duke, The Duchess and Mister Chang politely turned their backs and made pretence of examining something of urgent interest on the table. This diversion conveniently persisted for as long as the three girls made their new introductions.

Francesca and Genji endeavoured to link their pasts into their present, but it transpired that Janine's grasp of her personal history was more tenuous than they had realised.

Janine struggled to compare her memories with those of her two friends. She tried to piece together the real history that had elapsed, all those years ago, as opposed to the fraudulent recollections that tormented her. Eventually, Janine grew exasperated and declared that her most pressing and urgent need was to fully recover her memory.

Mister Chang sat her down, by the fire, and took the seat directly in front of her.

"Your Ladyship," Mister Chang said, looking earnest and sincere, "Your mind has memories that allow it to join up different genuine events in your life and steer it away from constantly gnawing at those things that are best left alone."

Janine nodded, but remained dubious and dissatisfied.

"You first came here as a tiny child. It was on a stormy night with the wind howling and the rain lashing down. It was the occasion of the first attempt on your life."

Janine's eyes widened, but she held her tongue.

"At first, it was thought that your enemies had found you completely by chance. It later emerged that you had been betrayed. Your would-be killers searched the cottage for you, but it was without success and they were forced to give up. Your nurse had run and hidden with you in a tiny secret chamber behind a false wall."

Janine raised her eyebrows at this, then knotted them. Mister Chang offered her an explanation.

"Such places were built, in the last century, for the purpose of sheltering priests during the years of religious persecutions. No matter how unusual it might be for such a small building, the knowledge of how to construct them was known."

Janine nodded.

"They ransacked the house and fled, hoping to be far away by the time that any alarm was raised. Their urgency to depart was not without good reason! They would likely have known that The Duke of Northumberland was in the region He was a long-time sympathiser of the Brydda and was notorious for his packs of tracking dogs that were called 'bloodhounds'."

Janine sat entranced by the tale, her eyes fixed in the distance, unaware of what might be before them.

"Once that kind of dog has the smell of a person in their noses, their quarry cannot escape them. It is only a matter of time before they are found. A group of The Duke of Northumberland's horsemen and a pack of a dozen bloodhounds were despatched and they ruthlessly hunted down the men who had been sent to kill you. It is said that the howling pack was set upon the men and that they tore them apart. They say that the dogs ate parts of the corpses."

Janine shivered at this information.

"The Brydda brought you here, to Brech Woorlach, frantic for a refuge and no longer able to know who they could trust and unsure where else you would be truly safe."

Mister Chang paused and made an almost imperceptible nod to The Duke. The Duke promptly took over the story.

"Your mother's closest and most trusted followers brought you here to Brech Woorlach. They took a chance that it might serve as a sanctuary for their cause. Your mother, in her youth, had saved the life of my grandfather. It was a selfless act of kindness for someone in desperate need. She had no inkling that he was a hugely rich and wealthy merchant, nor that, one day, he would become a duke. To honour my grandfather and to discharge, on his behalf, a debt of gratitude, I opened my doors to these unexpected callers."

Janine nodded, absorbing this information and mulling it over.

"Your mother had no idea where you had been taken. Only that you were safe at a trusted refuge. She agreed to give you up. It was the ultimate, heart-breaking sacrifice of a mother. She gave you up in order that you should survive to inherit her crown."

"No!" Janine protested, "My mother was a lowly woman of no status and humble means!"

"Your mother was Queen of the West," The Duke replied, "She was the rightful queen of the West Highlands."

Janine looked confused.

"Your mother tended to you in your early life, just like any mother might. She lived with you there, in that cottage, because it was a place that would raise no suspicions. Despite this, she was mindful of her enemies and of their growing strength. She was mindful of those amongst them who had allied themselves with foreign powers."

Janine looked serious and concerned.

"In the Winter she returned, alone, to her stronghouse at Fort Augustus. It was around this time that things grew still more dangerous. Careful to make life difficult for any ill-wishers, she moved from stronghouse to stronghouse across her domain, staying no more than a few days or a week with each of her lairds, before moving on."

Janine's face was deeply contemplative.

"When you were three years old, after two years of being away from you, your mother came to find you, here, at Brech Woorlach. She stayed through Spring and Summer and then left, taking you with her."

Janine nodded, slowly, as if this were somehow an event she recollected.

"Your mother disappeared from her role as Queen of the West, choosing instead, to return to the role she had previously adopted of a poor, struggling woman on a small holding. She lived with your father, a penniless but − I am absolutely certain − thoroughly good man."

"He was," Janine assured him, "He most definitely was."

"Then, when you were seven years old, your relative safety was disrupted. King James fell under the influence of people who were your enemies and they steered him towards the idea that the Queen of the West might be a threat to his rule. Those of the king's forces who were opposed to you, began a hunt to find you, and you were returned to the safety of Brech Woorlach."

Here, The Duke stopped and looked ill at ease. Janine looked up, sudden recognition illuminating her face.

"I last saw my mother when I was ten," Janine offered, barely managing to maintain her composure.

"Yes. That is when she was forced to flee and, fearing for your life, she sent the Brydda to bring you back to Brech Woorlach," The Duke confirmed.

"The Duke and I," The Duchess said, looking affectionately at him, "Did not simply give you a home, here. We and all our family made you a part of our lives."

Francesca nodded emphatically at this remark and smiled wistfully.

"You were with us from the age of seven until you were twelve, when...." Revealed The Duchess, before suddenly hesitating, "When events suddenly..."

"When suddenly," her husband interrupted, clenching his teeth and looking furious, "The Duke of Cumberland changed his allegiances! A move that cost the life of several good and worthy people, including my brother and my uncle."

The Duke and The Duchess looked at each other for a long moment and then The Duke turned back to Janine, as if some sort of agreement had been reached.

"I regret to tell you," The Duke advised, "That The Duke of Cumberland's treachery also cost the life of your mother."

"My mother is dead?" Gasped Janine.

The Duke's expression was one of grief and The Duchess looked visibly upset. They both nodded. Janine was too numbed to say anything and sat staring at the sun through the window.

"It was then that our plan was hatched," said Mister Chang.

Janine now understood why she was twelve years old when she had, for her own protection, been hidden away at Dunkeld Manor as a maid servant. The silence in the room that ensued was overwhelming.

"My husband sought out The Duke of Cumberland and killed him," The Duchess declared.

"Death was too good for him," The Duke complained.

The Duchess reached out and rested a hand on his arm.

"I killed him!" The Duke said, venomously, sitting very tall, "I killed him for you and for your mother."

"Cumberland was taken by surprise!" Remarked The Duchess, with a wicked smirk.

"He was indeed!" Confirmed The Duke, "I drew my pistol on him slowly and purposefully. At first, he looked confused. He stared at me, utterly shocked, for what felt like a minute but must have only been a few seconds."

The members of his audience smiled widely, already well familiar with the tale, but evidently relishing the retelling of it.

'My dear fellow!' said The Duke, making comic mockery of an aristocratic English accent, 'What on Earth can be the matter?'

His audience shrieked with laughter.

"I know everything!" The Duke narrated, quoting his own words.

The Duke of Cumberland solemnly interlocked the fingers of both hands, making a bridge on which he rested his chin.

"I knew him to be guilty, at once," The Duke of Bo'Ness confided, "In my experience, if somebody is completely innocent of any wrongdoing and you tell them that you 'know everything', they are totally bewildered. In fact, they are perplexed! The Duke of Cumberland, however, replied: *'I don't know what you're talking about.'*"

Mister Chang and Francesca shook their heads, clearly amused by the recounting of the Cumberland's blatant audacity.

"Not the words of an innocent man," The Duchess reproached.

"Absolutely!" Said The Duke, triumphantly.

"A scoundrel if I ever heard of one," The Duchess grinned.

"I said *'Maybe **this** will explain,'* and looked at him grimly, "The Duke recounted, "Then, I squeezed the trigger of my pistol and a lead ball the size of a thimble deposited itself between The Duke of Cumberland's eyes."

The was enthusiastic applause, accompanied by unrestrained guffaws and whoops.

The Duke leaned forward, confidentially, "He looked astonished!"

"And then ever so slightly dead!" His wife howled.

At this, his listeners dissolved into peals of laughter. Even Genji set aside her reserved disposition to join in. Janine also laughed, amused, not just by the tale and its telling, but by its gleeful reception.

With great interest Janine surreptitiously appraised the relationship between The Duke and The Duchess, noting the way they sat, the way they spoke and the way they behaved with each other. He was a powerful, intelligent and confident man. She was a refined, educated and accomplished woman of great talent, ability and personal merit. Their love for each other was manifest, but so was their deep friendship and, beyond this, their mutual respect. This, Janine decided, was something wonderful. It was a union of equals. A man and a woman at ease with each other's equivalent greatness.

Janine was unaware of quite what expression she may have had on her face, but The Duchess caught her unawares with a sudden turn of her head and saw her looking. It was almost as if she **knew** that she was being watched. Before Janine could adopt a more guarded and neutral visage, The Duchess gave her a knowing look and a very genuine smile.

Just as Janine felt a twinge of embarrassment, The Duchess bowed her head in deference. Janine raised her eyebrows, tilted her head to one side and gave her a thin, pursed lip smile of mock displeasure. In return, The Duchess gave her a wry grin, rocked her head side to side and then shrugged her shoulders. It appeared that, for The Duchess, learning not to bow would require some further practise.

"I was here until I was twelve. Is that so?" Janine asked The Duchess, encouraging her to continue her recollections.

"Yes, that's right. You were twelve when we discovered further treachery by The Duke of Cumberland's successor. It prompted us to wonder if there might have be more, undiscovered, traitors. So it was decided that you would be safest outside of these walls, somewhere that nobody would think to look for you."

Everybody nodded their heads wisely.

"In the end, we engaged the skills of Mister Chang to change your mind and alter your memories. This way, you could hide without raising any suspicion. It seemed the perfect way to remove any fear of you saying the wrong thing or acting incautiously. You would be unable to do so if you had no idea of your own identity."

There was more sombre nodding from everyone and the discussion passed to each, in turn, as they recalled their own part in the events being described.

"You were trained to defend yourself," Mister Chang declared, taking up the tale, "And this was an extremely good thing, but your amazing combat skills would have been guaranteed to attract immediate attention if you ever used them in front of witnesses. So, as a precaution, it was decided that you should only be allowed to use your knowledge of the martial arts if your life were in danger."

"Yes, I see," Janine said, "And I take it that I was also made to forget about such occurrences the moment they were over?"

"Indeed," Mister Chang agreed, "I gave your brain an instruction that your awareness – that is your conscious mind – should fade away into the background when you were in mortal danger and that your combat skills should come to the fore and take full control. It happened to be that I was eating breakfast, down here in these chambers, when I hit upon that idea. By chance, one of the servants had left a little bell on my tray, the kind used to summon assistance if I were seated upstairs in the breakfast room. I employed the sound of that bell as a mental trigger to tell you to yield to the fighter inside you and, effectively, to go to sleep until the danger was over."

Janine frowned, heavily, and felt a wave of sadness come over her.

"Yes," she said, "I remember the sound in my ears. I remember it distinctly. Hearing it would make me feel...." She hesitated as she searched for the words, "....strangely confused. I remember, too, that afterwards.... I would have the sensation of having woken, abruptly, from a dream that I couldn't recall."

Mister Chang looked chastened, but continued to listen without protest.

"The only way that my mind could make sense of it, and resume my grip on reality, was to presume that someone had miraculously intervened to rescue me from harm."

Janine thought for a moment, then gave a hollow, humourless laugh, "As it turns out, it was actually true! Though I would have never imagined that I was **both** people."

She shook her head and gave an ironic chuckle, "I used to look for them," she explained, "I thought that they must have hidden themselves or run away."

Mister Chang appeared agitated and looked at her timidly. She waved her hand at him, dismissively, to indicate that he need not worry further about the matter. Then, slowly descending into a pool of hazy memories, she stared vacantly into empty space.

"I am alive, still," she said, at last, "And it is due to your good offices. To you magnificent people. To my friends."

Mister Chang waited for a few moments and, when she did not speak further, he resumed his story.

"We found you a position as a servant with a laird at a stronghouse and..." Mister Chang began.

"And," The Duchess interrupted, "After much soul searching and desperate recrimination..."

Mister Chang looked relieved that she was willing to assert common blame for those events.

"We decided to simply let you be," The Duke finished.

The Duchess gave Janine the most heartbreakingly sad look of motherly love and adoration, her eyes misting up and her bottom lip trembling.

"They say that, sometimes, we have to be cruel to be kind," The Duke said, looking mournful.

"I am alive and I am here," Janine replied, kindly, giving each of them the absolution that they appeared to sorely need.

Francesca's guilt, however, was not appeased.

"It is most gracious of you, Your…." Said Francesca, suddenly pausing.

Janine knew that she had been about to address her as 'Your Majesty'.

"It is most gracious of Your Ladyship," Francesca resumed, "And most comforting that you do not condemn us, but – I am sorry to say – there are some who find it an agonisingly difficult thing to forgive themselves."

Janine's gaze at Francesca was unambiguously one of tenderness.

"I love you as my sister," Janine said gently, then – looking to Genji – added, "You, too, my precious friend."

Genji's face illuminated as if the sun had shone through it and she dropped her head to sob, silently. The Duchess reached across and drew Genji into her arms, as she had done, to Janine, at the dinner table. Genji relaxed into the embrace and cried without embarrassment. Janine deliberately moved her eyes elsewhere but, in a single heartbeat, her soul informed her that she – whether she be a queen or not – dearly loved The Duchess, too, and beyond anything that words could express.

Janine wondered what force of spirit occupied The Duchess that allowed her – as a refined and cultured member of the nobility – to hug a servant girl in that way and do so without shame or self-regard. Then, her mind flashed to the young Queen of the West who would – one day – become her mother, who cleaned and dressed the stinking wounds of a shipwrecked sailor.

After a couple of minutes, Genji managed to sufficiently recover herself to return to her own chair and sat dabbing her red eyes with a handkerchief. Francesca reached and put an arm around her shoulders and leaned to kiss her hair. Janine was moved by the love and affection of these people to the very pit of her being. Now, she finally understood how her mother could have left her child in their care. For their love was all pervading.

Janine wondered about her ancestor, Kiffan the Defiant, and imagined what incredible courage it must have taken and what overwhelming love for her people, that she could challenge a crowd of strong, muscular men – fleeing from the Vikings – to turn around and fight them. What kind of spirit must it have taken Kiffan, too, to give them that famous, heroic speech? The one that passed down in history and was so esteemed by The Brydda? She recalled the words.

'If you run today, then you condemn yourselves to run for the rest of your lives! You must fight them, here and now, or you must die a thousand times over in your nightmares, forever unable to repair the past and restore your honour.'

Janine knew that – in mind, if not in body – she had left the room and had shrunk away into the depths of her own thoughts, but she did not care to return.

Women, Janine reminded herself, were regarded in society as the lowest and most insignificant people. Women were shunned and belittled by men. They were scorned, humiliated, crushed and broken. They were treated as worthless possessions with no heed given to their feelings or their self-respect. It was even worse so, back in the times of Kiffan! Yet, Kiffan had not just beseeched and implored those men. She had rebuked them. She had condemned them. Then, in outrageous impudence, she had commanded them! Kiffan had commanded them to follow her and they had obeyed! She had famously run at the Vikings with her sword drawn and held high, and these warriors had turned and run after her – run **with** her – to attack their foes!

The Vikings must have been astonished! They must, in fact, have been completely astounded! They must have found it difficult to believe the evidence of their own eyes! The Vikings had, previously, driven their enemy before them like a farm girl herding chickens, holding her apron wide and flapping it! The Vikings had harried their foes as they bolted, slaying the ones who fell behind. They had called after them with vile insults. Then, in an inexplicable moment of fate, their enemy had stopped, turned around, and charged at them with a frenzied, wild ferocity they had never anticipated!

This courageous woman. This woman whose blood flowed, today, through Janine's own veins. This woman of her own line. Janine wanted to make her ancestor proud. She vowed that she would set her hand to the plough that was her fate and that she would not remove it until whatever was required of her was complete.

Returning her attention to the room, Janine's mind suddenly engaged, again, with those around her. She looked at The Duchess, who smiled radiantly back at her.

This woman and this man – The Duke and The Duchess – had taken Janine in when the price they might have had to pay was the destruction of their lives, their home and their fortune. An army — if they had suspected their disloyalty — could have easily taken battering rams to their doors, wrecked them, and torn through the house, desecrating it and, perhaps, even setting fire to it. They would have dragged The Duke and The Duchess out onto the lawn, thrown a rope over the branch of a tree and hung them both as traitors. Worse, still, they might have piled logs around a post and burned them both at the stake. They were heroes. They had adopted her when she was in complete and utter desolation. They had taken in an orphan child and given her a family to love her.

Janine stood and walked slowly and carefully over to where The Duchess sat. The Duchess looked up at her, uncertainly. Janine bent forward and extended her arms to fold her into them and The Duchess tentatively moved to accept the embrace. Janine knelt by the woman's chair and hugged her with all her might and pressed her head against her shoulder.

"My second mother!" Janine sobbed.

The Duchess wept unrestrained, sobbing and choking on her happiness. Janine reached out an arm and beckoned the Duke to come to her and he moved to join their embrace.

"My second father!" She declared.

CHAPTER 33

Burberry continued to look contemplative, staring into the middle distance with a mind unhindered by the distraction of what was around him. Presently, he emerged from his reverie and began to shake his head, wearily.

"I am bound for Inverness," he declared, "There, at the Fortress, I am instructed to investigate information supplied in confidence to the crown."

Alex and Hamish traded wary glances.

"A secret despatch from the King, relating to this matter, was intercepted between Perth and Pitlochry," Burberry continued, his voice dropping lower "The document was related to the identity of the Queen of the West. Or should I say *Queens* of the West? That is if the rumours circulating in certain circles are to be believed."

Alex and Hamish looked intrigued.

"There are whispers of two women who claim the title," Burberry confided, "The Campbells would have us believe that one of them is an imposter, intended to cast doubt on the succession."

"But which one?" asked Hamish.

Burberry shook his head, "That is part of what I have been sent to Inverness to discover."

"Stealing a letter from the king is an almost unthinkable crime!" said Alex.

"Aye," the constable agreed, "It is common knowledge that to harass or interfere with a courier carrying a Royal Mail is punishable by immediate execution on capture."

"Waylaying a Royal Mail is a crime normally beneath even the most hardened criminal," Hamish pointed out.

"Aye, it is," replied Burberry, "It is regarded as a shameful thing. It would bring disgrace upon the local laird, whether they were acting for him or not, and it grievously sully their reputation for all time."

Hamish nodded his agreement and Alex nodded, too.

"I know a lot about the journey of a letter," Burberry announced, "I was, in fact, a courier myself for many a year."

Alex and Hamish appeared impressed.

"A letter from London to Edinburgh," Burberry declared, "Makes it as far as Cambridge on the first day, to Lincoln on the second day, to York on the third, to Durham on the fourth, to Carter Bar on the England-Scotland border on the fifth and to Edinburgh on the sixth. A letter to Perthshire takes another day. Had it been sent by the king's personal service, of course, it would have taken half that time, as the riders would have travelled through the night."

His audience of two nodded their heads in appreciation of his knowledge.

"The couriers travelling North and South meet each other at defined points, known as stages. It is where they await the arrival of their opposite number. The courier who is heading North exchanges his mail bag with the courier heading South.

"The bags change hands on a strictly face-to-face basis and both men ensure that the lock, chain and seal are intact before they hand them over. These are serving military men, but they may as well be in the priesthood for their obsessive dedication to their duty. They work in absolutely any weather and, when their schedule dictates, they work on Sunday – the Lord's Day – despite it being the day of rest."

"Just like sailors!" quipped Hamish.

"And soldiers!" Added Alex.

"The service can be considered to be as secure as any kind of human endeavour could ever possibly be."

"But…" offered Alex, sensing the word hanging in the air.

"But, as long as we employ human beings and not angels, there is always a potential for things to happen that were not intended to happen."

"And," Alex enquired, "You also know *this* to be a fact, too?"

"Indeed I do!" laughed the constable, "For there is an inn at Carter Bar where lodges a strikingly beautiful woman – with a body like the figurehead at the bow of a sailing ship – who has proven to be a distraction utterly irresistible to even the most resolute of men."

Alex and Hamish applauded.

"There just so happens to be another lodger, there, who is an extremely skilled thief and pickpocket," Burberry declared with an exaggerated wink, "He is a criminal with an astonishing gift! He is able to remember, faultlessly and in precise detail, absolutely any document he has seen. His recollection is as clear as if he were still holding it in his hands."

Alex and Hamish applauded, again.

"I had installed, in the room of the lady I mentioned, a very impressive and robust iron trunk with an equally impressive and robust lock. She pretends that it is an heirloom of great sentimental value and declares it to be resistant to any kind of tampering. While they are enjoying the pleasure of her company, the couriers are invited to store their mail bag in it. They are even encouraged to add their own lock for extra reassurance. Such is her allure, that they always more than willing to comply."

Alex and Hamish looked puzzled. Burberry smirked in response.

"This seemingly impregnable trunk, however, has an ingeniously hidden door in its base. This is accessible from a crawl space, underneath the floorboards, which can be accessed by her accomplice in the room next door."

The three men laughed and the constable, holding his sides, managed to fight off the need to groan with pain from his injuries.

"The combined talents of these two people, whom I retain in my employment on generous terms, are extremely productive. They allow me to know what is going on in official circles with a great degree of reliability. This is the reason I know that the letter that was intercepted between Perth and Pitlochry was conveyed by a special rider and not in the normal manner."

Alex and Hamish nodded, slowly and thoughtfully.

"Whatever was in that letter," Burberry remarked, dryly, "It was worth somebody risking dangling from a tree by their neck!"

"Perhaps its contents were the reason that they were equally bold in attacking a constable," Alex added.

"The McCarthys are the prime suspects for intercepting the King's letter," the constable observed, "And for the murder of the man who carried it... but they have taken knowledge of whatever was contained in it down to the Pits of Hell with them."

Alex told the horses to walk on and they did.

"Do you think they destroyed the letter or sent it on to somebody else?" Asked Alex.

"I have a feeling that the answer to that question is what I am going to find out in Inverness," replied Burberry.

"I don't want to worry you," Hamish warned Burberry, "But if the people you are up against have already made attempts on your life, they are certain to try again. You would be wise to keep those troops of yours close at hand for the rest of your journey."

"I will," Burberry assured him, "I will."

The constable drew in a deep breath and then let it out again, in several protracted instalments, pausing to moan a little as he went.

"I only took the risks I did in order to draw the McCarthys out," he explained, after recovering himself enough to talk.

Hamish was astonished!

"What! Are you serious?" Hamish boomed, furiously, "You wanted to 'draw them out'? Well, you certainly succeeded in doing that! You also almost succeeded in getting yourself killed in the process!"

Constable Burberry looked shamefaced. Nobody had said it, but there was the unmistakable suggestion that Alex and Hamish could have died, too. There was a long, uncomfortable silence. It was, eventually, broken by Alex.

"Everybody in these parts will be massively grateful, I am sure, for the demise of those brutal thugs that were the McCarthys," he told Burberry, in measured tones, "And whatever events occurred to bring that about, the locals will regard it as a blessing. Even if that, and that alone, had been the only thing achieved, today, then you deserve a medal for it."

Burberry nodded, forlornly, and Hamish scowled and shrugged his shoulders begrudgingly.

"I can't say that preserving my own life was the thing at the front of my mind when I came up here, after you," Hamish declared, "It was, firstly, my outrage at the thought that the McCarthys might be involved in your disappearance and, secondly, your astonishing boldness...."

At this, Burberry gave him an old fashioned look through narrowed eyes and Hamish finally smiled.

"We'll call it your 'boldness' for the sake of argument," Hamish offered, amiably, "Though, of course, other words do come readily to mind!"

The three men hooted with laughter, Burberry hugging his sides and yelping, while Alex and Hamish slapped their thighs and patted each other's backs. The tension broken and good relations restored, the rest of the journey was soon over and – in no time at all – the wagon pulled off the road and rolled to a halt in front of the inn.

Caitlan Pottle came rushing out and embraced her husband, sobbing with relief for his safe return. She then proceeded to hug Alex until he could hardly breathe and kissed Burberry fervently on both cheeks.

With a few extra helpers, they managed to get Constable Burberry out of the wagon and up the stairs to his room. Laid, at last, on the sumptuously comfortable bed, he moaned loudly and at length, but *this* time as much from pleasure as from pain.

Caitlan despatched the stable lad to fetch the healer from the village of Killiecrankie and the boy was over the moon to be allowed to drive the wagon, alone. Hamish instructed him to fetch back a pig to roast and a side of beef, too, and instructed the yard man to dig a pit and stack up firewood in it for a celebration roast.

There was great relief that they had all three returned safely and, as expected, the news that the much hated McCarthys had been wiped out was, without exception, received with glee.

Hamish called the stable lad back, just as he had set off, and gave him an additional errand. He was instructed to find Captain McCleary in the forest and give him five crates of ale and half a dozen bottles of whisky from the store room. He was also to buy a pair of pigs for them to roast. Burberry insisted on splitting the cost with Hamish and wouldn't take 'no' for an answer.

Once everything had settled down at the inn, Alex and Hamish took a bottle of whisky up to Burberry and poured out generous glasses for them all. Hamish and Burberry sat on the bed, while Alex sat in the armchair, in the corner.

Raising his glass, Hamish proposed a toast: "To a successful journey to Schnecky," he proposed, using the slang name for Inverness, "And may we all return safely and unscathed!"

"We?" Cried Burberry, taken by surprise.

"Yes!" Hamish confirmed, "That's right. We!"

Hamish beamed at the constable and folded his arms across his chest in defiance.

"Just so," Alex declared, raising his glass for a second time, "We are coming with you!"

Ewan Burberry, realising that the two of them had already agreed this plan between them, looked from Hamish Pottle to Alex Brennan with a stern expression on his face. The two men looked back, eager, earnest and determined. Burberry pursed his lips in a rueful smile and blew a derisory puff of air through them to declare his vexation.

"I hope you both know what you're doing?" The constable admonished.

The two men appeared to be in no mood to discuss the matter and maintained a stony silence. They had announced, flatly, that they would accompany him to Inverness and that, it would seem, was that.

"You're both crazy!" Burberry told them and grimaced.

With difficulty, Burberry began to shuffle himself further up the bed. The moment he started to move, Alex and Hamish sprang to their feet and insisted on helping him. It was clear that his injuries from his clash with the McCarthys were extensive and were continuing to cause him substantial pain and discomfort. With great care his two comrades gently eased him up the pile of pillows until his head was almost touching the top board. The patient winced and groaned but put on a brave face. Next, they puffed up and repositioned his pillows and drew the covers fully up to his chin.

"If you like," Hamish offered, with a wink, "We can all step outside and settle any disagreement, regarding us accompanying you to Schnecky, with a stick fight or perhaps a couple of laps of the field."

Constable Burberry cringed at the suggestion and managed a gruff laugh, before throwing the covers back to free his arms.

"I think you'll be laid up here for a couple of days before you'll be anything like fit to travel," Hamish announced.

Burberry nodded, wearily, and sighed.

"They took quite a dislike to you!" Alex remarked, eyeing the constable's cuts and bruises with a twinkle in his eye.

"They had no regard, at all, for my welfare," Burberry confided, "If they were running an inn, I would never visit their establishment again!"

"Oh! Really?" Hamish said in mock surprise, "And there was I, just making arrangements for you to be tied to the pump and flogged in the morning! I try to make my guests' stay, here, as much to their liking as possible!"

Burberry mostly suppressed a groan and put a hand to his injured ribs.

"I'll be taking my custom elsewhere, if there are no barbs on the tails of that whip, innkeeper!"

There was a cursory tap at the door and Caitlan came in, carrying a tray with broth, oat cakes, butter and several hunks of hot toasted bread with cream and thick jam.

Caitlan busied herself about the task of raising the constable still further up and propping his pillows behind him to her own satisfaction. Then she fussed over the blankets and the quilt until they were aligned to her own exacting standards.

Putting a broad, flat cushion on her patient's lap, she then placed the tray on top of it and balanced it carefully. Taking one of Alex' hands, she placed it on the edge of the tray to hold it steady. Alex obediently held on to it and Burberry caught his eye with a flash of amusement.

They all sat and watched, in amiable silence, as Ewan Burberry demolished the meal and wiped his mouth with the cotton kerchief from the tray. Caitlan took the tray to the door and reached out onto the landing, from where she retrieved a second, smaller tray, which she brought back to the bed.

"I did not know if it would be cocoa or something a wee bit stronger you might be wanting," she declared, wickedly.

Burberry unleashed his amazing smile and the room seemed to brighten and sparkle with a mysterious warmth. He motioned to the stone beaker of whisky she held and shrank back his head in an imitation of shyness. Caitlan smirked and passed the beaker to him, nonetheless. The constable emptied the beaker in three gulps and closed his eyes to enjoy the welcome fiery warmth of the whisky as it flooded through him.

Burberry settled back into his pillows, but only part way, as if to indicate that there was still formal business to be conducted.

"Some brave things need to be done by a man," Burberry began, "And some brave things need to be done by a woman. Any man holding a musket or a sword and thinking that he is braver than a woman is sorely wrong and deeply misguided. There are acts of bravery by a woman that are more excruciating than most men can know."

Caitlan narrowed her eyes suspiciously at the constable for a moment.

"You're telling me that you're taking my husband to Inverness."

Her words were not a question.

"Taking," Burberry repeated, as if toying with the word and testing it on his lips, "I'd not say 'taking' so much."

"Oh! Would you not?" She asked, pointedly looking with dark disapproval at Hamish.

Hamish looked at her sullenly but said nothing.

"He will, it seems, be accompanying me on the journey," Burberry advised.

Caitlan remained silent and nobody else spoke. The aura of goodness and peace in the room was not dispelled. If anything, it increased. Caitlan gazed down at her fingers, which were frantically knotting and unknotting the corner of her apron. Suddenly, she looked up and locked eyes with Burberry.

"You said **the words**," she said, accusingly, "You said them in Alex' ear when the two of you were sitting by the fire out the back."

It was clear to Burberry that there were no secrets, here, between husband and wife. Burberry smiled again, with great sadness this time, and the atmosphere of joy and contentment in the room grew yet stronger still.

"**She** is in danger," Burberry proclaimed.

Nobody in the room had even a flicker of doubt that he was referring to the Queen of the West.

"And will this endeavour require the life of my husband and of this heroic young man," Caitlan asked, her voice quiet and restrained, "And maybe yours, too?"

Burberry's face became suddenly older and an overwhelming melancholy gripped his features. As they waited for his reply, a single tear spilled from his eye and rolled down his cheek.

"If it did, would you hold us back?"

Caitlan's lip trembled and tears began to trickle down her own face. Very slowly and deliberately and with heart-breaking sorrow, she shook her head. After a few moments she breathed in, deeply, fully inflating her lungs, and raised her head straight and level.

"There is no Scotland without England and there is no England without Scotland," she said, emphatically, quoting the words of Brydda folklore, "For they are like two fingers, one next to the other, wrapped around each other."

Caitlan held up her hand and, extending her first two fingers, crossed left over right and then right over left.

"We have two hands," she quoted, holding her own hands with palms up, "Yet we cannot wash either one of them, without the other."

She looked at her hands, reproachfully, then threw them up in disgust and let them fall to her lap.

"And how else would we ever tie a bow?" She asked.

Hamish made a muffled snort of disdain and followed it with a rumbling noise in his chest.

"Yet we kill each other, from time to time. I kill yours and you kill mine," said Hamish, quoting the famous poem.

Alex smiled, for he knew exactly the lines that Hamish was about to say and took up the words for him.

"But God help he who kills a Scot, in the sight of the English! Fool! Do not! Nor kill the English in a Scotsman's sight. For dead as a stone will be your plight!"

Burberry smiled. These, he knew, were the famous rhymes of old Noory McGregor from over a hundred years ago. The man who, as legend would have it, lived in two tiny houses at Carter Bar, sharing a common wall between them with a connecting door and built to span the border – as it was at that time – between England and Scotland. Noory boasted that he lived in England in a morning and would walk through to next door to live in Scotland from Noon until Midnight.

Burberry finished the quotation for him.

"We reserve the right to kill each other, most jealously, as if a lover! With fury are we zealots prone, to hold this right to be our own!"

While nobody was in the mood to laugh, they managed a reluctant attempt at it. Alex reached down and ostentatiously shook and straightened his kilt. Then, slapping the material against his thigh, he cleared his throat to speak.

"But, all this said and agreed, I've never seen an Englishman look even half as bonny as **this** sporting a tartan about him!"

This time, they all laughed for real. By unspoken common consent, it was decided that Constable Burberry should be allowed to rest, now. They gathered at his side to wish him a pleasant night. Outside, the skies were starting to darken and the first faint red blush of dusk was making itself apparent. Their pleasantries completed, they marched to the door. They were just about to step into the hall when Burberry called to them.

"When we first became acquainted, I told you that I had killed the elder of the McCarthys and that he was over the saddle of my pack horse."

He paused, but no reply or comment came in response.

"I never told you how come I was able to make off with their father's body, to sling it on my horse."

Hamish reached out and took hold of the handle of the door and placed his thumb down on the flat pan of the lever used to lift the latch. He stood still, frozen to the spot. He didn't want to know the answer to this question. It chilled his blood to contemplate it. It had certainly been a brazen act. Eventually, he lifted the latch and exited. As he pulled the door closed, he stopped and reluctantly replied through the narrow gap.

"You are an enemy of the McCarthys. You are an enemy of the queen's enemies. We presumed you would tell us in your own good time."

Hamish pulled the door closed and let the latch fall. He had not looked back to Burberry, but he knew that there was a smile on his face. He did not need to see it to know that it was there.

Caitlan, Hamish and Alex filed down the narrow stairs, descending through its helter-skelter curve, and emerged into the hall between the kitchen and the bar room.

They heard loud approaching footsteps and a man appeared in the doorway to the bar. He wore the army uniform of the Lothian Pikes and Muskets and doffed his cap to Caitlan.

"A good afternoon to you," Caitlan said, bowing to acknowledge his courtesy.

"I have news for the constable," replied the soldier.

"He is resting," Hamish told him.

"The news is urgent," insisted the soldier.

"He is injured and needs his rest to recover," Caitlan intervened.

"The news is urgent," repeated the man.

"Just how urgent can this news be that you need to get a man from his sick bed?" Caitlan snapped.

The soldier stood tall and put out his chin.

"The Campbells have attacked…" He declared, before pausing awkwardly, unsure of what more it would be appropriate to say, then added: "They have attacked **her**."

He did not venture to explain who he might mean by "her". It was clear that he was not going to risk telling them anything further. It was clear, too, that he was unsure how much they might already know.

"Where?" Asked Alex.

The soldier frowned and did not reply. Instead, he shuffled and looked awkward. Hamish realised that there would definitely be no more information forthcoming from him man and, with some reluctance, he relented.

"He's upstairs. I'll take you," said Hamish.

Hamish started off back up the stairs and the soldier duly followed, with Alex and Caitlan tagging along behind.

Burberry had not gone to sleep and lay awake, staring at the ceiling, watching the golden light of the sun wavering and shimmering on the white lime between the black beams.

On entering the room, the soldier stood to attention and saluted. The constable weakly returned the salute. There was a brief, uneasy silence before Burberry told the soldier that he could speak openly and then, irritably, insisted that he did. The soldier looked at the others in the room a little uncertainly, but – when urged – was able to find his tongue and read, with little enthusiasm, from a roll of paper.

'This morning a large number of troops opposed to the woman known as 'The Queen of the West', launched attacks on her forces, at Boat of Garten, striking simultaneously from the North and South,' the document revealed, *'We believe that she was there to perform a ceremony defining the border of her territory, along the far bank of the Spey. Informants tell us that her people had received warnings of likely bloodshed and, in response, the Clan MacDonald had sent an armed escort to accompany her, which included around thirty cavalrymen.'*

Hamish and Alex looked completely aghast, unable to believe their ears. This soldier, from one of the Scottish brigades, appeared to be puzzlingly familiar with the movements and activities of the Queen of the West!

This, on the other hand, appeared to come as no shock to Constable Burberry, who only registered surprise at the mention of cavalry. Sitting up straighter, he held out his hand and waved for the soldier to give him the document. Burberry cast his eye over the words on the paper, his eyebrows rising a couple of times and his mouth turning downward. After a short while, he handed it back to the soldier and told him to continue reading from where he had left off.

'Our scouts were unable to properly identify the attackers approaching from the North. Their tartans were many and varied and it is believed that they used a wide range of captured or stolen kilts and cloaks to disguise themselves. She crossed with only a light, token force, but had her full cavalry hidden close by.'

"Now, this **next** bit is something of a surprise!" Chirped Burberry with a roguish grin.

'The queen's soldiers did not come under any kind of assault from the Clan Grant forces during this whole time,' the soldier announced, his eyes widening as he took in the words, *'The Grants engaged the opposing force, side by side, with the queen's army.'*

"What!" Gasped Hamish, in disbelief.

"They are sworn enemies!" Alex exclaimed, equally perplexed.

"King James will be most interested in this information!" Burberry beamed, rubbing his hands in exaggerated glee.

"I can hardly believe my ears!" Hamish gasped.

"We are informed, most reliably, that the woman known as 'Queen of the West' did **not**, however, accept the pledge of the Laird Grant's sword," the soldier announced.

Hamish, Alex and Caitlan all exchanged puzzled glances.

"That point was made most clear by our spy," the constable reaffirmed, then quickly clapped his hand over his mouth and feigned a gasp, "I'm so sorry! I meant our lookouts!" He chuckled, "That's right, isn't it, soldier?"

"Yes, Sir!" Replied the soldier, ignoring the humour.

"We don't **spy** on the Queen of the West!" Burberry grinned, shaking his head in mock horror, "Of **course** we don't!"

The soldier, at pains to remain formal, said nothing.

"Carry on," Burberry instructed, looking at the man apologetically.

The soldier cleared his throat and continued.

'The woman was unhurt and, once the opposing army had been subdued, she moved back across the river with her troops and joined the second conflict to the South. The attacking army had a mixture of more recognisable clans, though there were still a lot of obviously false tartans being worn. Our lookouts were able to name them as being Campbells.'

"No surprise, there!" Burberry hooted.

'A little over an hour after the start of the conflict, a second wave of MacDonald troops arrived, coming across the mountains, and our....' the soldier paused and looked to Burberry before continuing, *'Our **lookouts**,'* the soldier said, placing special emphasis on the word, *'Were compelled to withdraw to safety, at this point, to avoid being seen and taken prisoner.'*

"Is the queen unharmed?" Asked Hamish.

The soldier looked at him with the vaguest glimmer of hostility in his gaze.

"I'm asking for no particular reason!" Hamish added, quickly.

"We are awaiting a further report," The soldier replied, testily.

Constable Burberry gave the man a cool, measured look and he appeared to falter and lose a couple of inches in height.

"The captain has concerns," the soldier advised, now looking a little contrite, "About what might happen if we remain here, now that there are defeated Campbell troops heading back home and likely to pass close by this location."

"He is worried for my safety?" Burberry queried, tilting his head to one side and fixing the man with narrowed eyes, "And yet I have a detachment of armed troops to escort me."

The soldier looked distinctly unsettled and nobody was in any doubt that he knew more than he was saying.

"They are Scotland's finest," Burberry added.

At this the soldier promptly stood tall and struck a dignified pose. Burberry was kind enough not to smile.

"The captain has made his despatch to Colonel MacPhail at Perth, reporting our own news of the recent...." The soldier hesitated and looked pained, as though the words had a bad taste, "Recent events. The things that have happened. The goings on."

"The McCarthys abducting me and my almost ending up dead?"

"Yes, Sir. Those events."

"Okay...." Burberry said, coaxing him to continue.

"Colonel MacPhail fears that a military presence here might be drawn into conflict with passing Campbells to no useful gain."

"So he wants to drag me out of my sick bed, sling me on a horse, and get me away from here as soon as possible?"

"Yes, Sir," replied the soldier, looking sheepish, "He would like you and your troops to depart urgently."

"If you will excuse me, then, I will just throw a handstand against the wall, cartwheel down the hall and then descend the stairs two at a time."

The soldier stood to attention in glum silence and allowed the attempt at comedy to wash over him. Burberry sighed a heavy sigh and lowered his head with a hand on his brow.

"Tell your comrades not to spare the hay in that wagon, then, soldier," the constable mused, "For I'll need most of this year's harvest between me and those boards."

The soldier mumbled an apologetic response and begged leave to go. He exited the door with the gratitude of a man granted parole on a life prison sentence.

Burberry moaned and placed his arm across his eyes.

"I have half a mind to stay here and let the Campbells hack me into a dozen pieces," he gasped, "For it might be a kinder and less painful way to depart this world than being bounced to death in the back of that wagon!"

"It could be that Colonel MacPhail has learned of your allegiances," Hamish laughed, "And he wants to do away with you with the maximum possible pain and discomfort!"

Burberry's mood deteriorated rapidly.

"We live in dangerous times!" He said, pretending to smile.

"I have a feeling that these times will grow more dangerous before they improve," Alex replied.

The constable sat, staring vacantly for a while, preoccupied by his thoughts.

"My father and my grandfather were both close acquaintances of The Duke of Moy," Burberry confided, looking bleakly nostalgic, "As a boy, many was the Brydda 'traitor' that I rowed across to the little island, in the middle of the loch, to live out their days in its prison."

Burberry gave a low chuckle before resuming.

"Many, too, were the times that I went back and rowed them to freedom, again, switching them for some monk or priest, who was only too eager to become their substitute and avail themselves of that blissful solitude and seclusion."

He gave another chuckle.

"The Duke very nearly had his own monastery over there!"

Everyone laughed.

"I have no eagerness to give up the bliss of this bed any earlier than the morning," Burberry announced, "Retreating Campbells or no retreating Campbells."

"I'll have some more whisky sent up to you," Caitlan told Burberry, "I have a feeling that you'll find it a welcome aid to sleep, tonight!"

"Send him the entire bottle!" Hamish mused, "The less he is able to feel in the morning, the better he'll travel!"

Burberry kissed Caitlan's hand and shook those of Hamish and Alex and told them that he looked forward to seeing them at first light.

His little party of visitors filed out once more and he slumped back into his pillows.

His mind raced with a hundred different thoughts and he felt sure that he would, indeed, be needing the help of the whisky, for the soldier had given him a secret signal. It indicated news that he thought he had better not share with Hamish and Alex, at least for the time being.

CHAPTER 34

Balgair stared at the shattered body of the eagle for a prolonged moment and then quickly made the sign of the cross, touching his fingers to his forehead, sternum and each shoulder.

"Move! Quickly! Everybody!" Gavin shouted, "Get her into the body sling and let's get off this hill!"

There was sudden, frenetic movement and Annis found herself deposited into the canvas sling with more urgency than care. She clenched her teeth against the pain and refused to cry out. She found herself becoming lightheaded and dizzy. Closing her eyes, she counted to ten and, when she opened them again, she heard Wild Flower's voice, soft and concerned.

"She has lost a lot of blood. Her mind will not work properly until she has had plenty to drink and a good long rest."

"We must get her to safety," said another, "When we have her somewhere we can protect her, she can begin to recover."

Annis recognised this as Gavin's voice.

"Guard her close!" A third person said, their voice tinged with desperate concern.

Annis tried to think, but she couldn't identify the voice. Something in the back of her disturbed mind told her that it was her mother.

"Is my mother here?" Annis asked, her voice slurred.

"Your mother?" Asked one of her attendants.

Somebody's face came close to her own and they spoke with tender reassurance.

"Everyone close to you is here."

Annis furrowed her brow in concentration, trying to make sense of this reply. Her thoughts refused to obey her, so she gave up and slumped back against the canvas. On the spur of the moment, she leaned up again and asked a question.

"Am I alive?" She asked.

"Yes, Your Majesty!" Somebody gasped, "Thank God and his angels, you are!"

She felt a jolt and then a swaying sensation as the horses set off. They were being urged along and were staggering and slipping as their hooves fought for traction.

It was clear that the animals were disconcerted, finding it difficult to adapt themselves to the way they had been harnessed. They seemed to be under the impression, from the feel of their parallel harnesses, that they were drawing a carriage, but neither horse could feel the rearward tug of such a device. Instead, while they were constrained to move side by side, there was a wooden cage of lashed poles between them, and they appeared to be finding the rigidity of it a challenge.

After a minute or so, much to Annis' relief, the two horses seemed to resolve their dilemma and were able to adopt a fast trot. Annis managed to smile. Horses, she told herself, were every bit as clever as people and some of them a lot more so!

Even with the buffeting and rolling, Annis still found herself alternately passing out and regaining consciousness. She moved between the two states so frequently that she was unsure which she occupied at any particular moment.

Annis could hear the voice of Wild Flower and presumed that she must be in the canvas hammock with her. If she had been able to focus her eyes, the queen would have seen Wild Flower standing astride the sling, gripping the saddle of the horse at either side.

It was evident to Annis, during her lucid moments, that Wild Flower could see ahead of them, as she kept giving the horses instructions. They would speed up, slow down, stop, go around objects and, occasionally, clamber over things, in response to her words. The soldier who was officially in charge of her conveyance had given up trying to command the horses and had yielded, reluctantly, to the good offices of this little girl.

They kept going for what seemed like an age and Annis eventually found herself in a state of delirium, neither awake nor asleep. She was distraught to find that – whatever her phase of mental awareness – she could always feel the swaying and buffeting of the sling between the horses.

She closed her eyes and reached out to the horses with her mind. Her mother had said, when she was a child, that horses had as much ability to be spiritual as people. She also said that horses were twice as likely as humans to be kind and good.

The horses, she felt, were anxious. She had learned to grit her teeth when the motion over rough ground caused her pain and this seemed to put the people who watched over her at peace. The horses, however, were not so easily fooled. She could feel their distress whenever the shaking and jolting caused her pain.

Annis reached up and placed her hand on the flank of the horse to her left. In reply, she felt a wave of love flow over her. She touched the other horse and felt the same. She closed her eyes, again, and as she drifted back into the darkness, she told them that they were doing a good job and that they should not fret. She couldn't explain how she knew, but the horses somehow felt happier.

CHAPTER 35

Annis became aware of them stopping and could feel people untying ropes from the body sling. Next, she felt herself being slowly lowered out of the apparatus. She became aware of something soft around her and realised that she had been transferred into a blanket. Annis could tell, from the movement, that she was being carried and, seeing the view above her darken, she knew that they were entering a building.

Before long, Annis could vaguely make out lamps or lanterns around her, illuminating the interior and she felt herself being laid onto a straw bed. She could smell the straw in the mattress and was pleased to note that it was fresh. Hazily, she became conscious of someone checking her wounds and then felt her dressings being changed.

There were people around her discussing her health in hushed voices. Someone leant over her and tentatively asked her questions. She felt bad for disappointing them by failing to answer. She could not make her tongue work. It wasn't long before she was drifting back off into a woozy, dreamless sleep.

"She **will** survive?" Balgair asked, a keen edge of fear in his voice.

"She **should** survive," replied Wild Flower, matching his emphasis on the vital word.

Balgair looked dismal and she decided to give him at least a little hope.

"She is young. She is extremely fit. She is in very good health. She has a strong mind. Those are all things that are going to help her recover."

"I should have seen the spearman!" Balgair exclaimed.

"No! You shouldn't!" Gavin responded in a disgusted tone.

"I wasn't paying enough attention to her safety."

"You are wrong. You were definitely paying attention. There were lots of things going on. You had a lot to do."

Balgair silently fumed and went quiet for a minute, brooding on his actions, reliving each and every moment before the spear was thrown.

"The strength of a chain...." Balgair began, his attention suddenly back in the room.

"Depends on its weakest link," Gavin finished for him.

"I was..." Balgair began.

"**You** were a strong part of the chain," Gavin intervened, "The only weakness was you being a human being and not a god from ancient myths or some impossible hero from a storybook."

Balgair whirled on Gavin and gave him a look like thunder.

"If you **had** been at fault," Gavin snarled, "You can be certain that I would not hide it from you! I would let you know the truth of it. I would not hold back my words!"

Balgair's rage simmered and he glowered savagely at anybody who dared to look in his direction.

A thought unexpectedly popped into Gavin's head. He turned abruptly to Balgair and looked into his eyes with complete calm. Balgair was taken by surprise at his sudden change of manner.

"The eagle!" Gavin blurted, "It came like a bolt from the blue!"

Balgair made a harsh guttural sound in agreement.

"It was a miracle," Wild Flower said blankly.

Gavin opened his mouth to disagree, but then found himself unable to actually dispute the statement. There was no other explanation for what had happened.

"Why would her life be saved by a miracle on the battlefield, if she were destined to die, later on, away from it?" Gavin asked, directing his question at Wild Flower.

"If you find yourself able to explain God's thinking and actions, you need to write and inform the heads of all the religions on Earth, without delay…." She replied with a sneering sarcasm far beyond her modest years.

Gavin and Balgair both shot her a disapproving look, but could not sustain them when they saw the sweet, cherubic smile on her face.

"Nature cares nothing for our concerns," Wild Flower confided, "Be it with or without holy assistance, what will happen, will happen. The only thing we can do is to wait for our fate to arrive."

Both men grunted their acceptance and looked completely empty. Wild Flower could feel their pain, their grief and their utter desolation.

"Each day of my life," she whispered, "Is like a week of life for anybody else in this mortal realm."

Gavin and Balgair both immediately tensed, knowing these words to be shameless blasphemy, but they did not respond.

"I feel that a force has been sent to assist her that is beyond anything we can possibly imagine. If this force is from God, then so be it. I bend my knee to Him. If this force is from before the existence of the world and before the beginning of time, when all things still dwelt in darkness, then so be it. The force of which I speak exists because God does not prevent it from existing. He allows it to be."

The two men began to raise their heads, to share a glance, but both thought better of it and returned their eyes to the floor.

"In that field, by the Spey, when our queen agreed to be baptised again in its waters, we all saw something and we all felt something. An eagle came and brought to her a ring that had been lost for around eight hundred years. We were all bathed in an energy that was intoxicating. The bird that fell to save her on the battlefield could do nothing else. Whatever is needed will occur because it has no option but to occur. If you toss a coin, you could talk long into the night about whether it will fall heads or heels, but you cannot influence the outcome. Let's just wait and see. What will be, will be."

"You speak the truth," said Gavin, solemnly.

"Aye, for sure you do," confirmed Balgair.

Wild Flower bent forward and kissed the ring on Queen Annis' finger. It did not flicker or flash and no flames erupted, but there was an instant aura of overpowering peace and wellbeing and nobody worried or fretted any more.

CHAPTER 36

Annis woke with a start. She felt cautiously around her and had the sensation of wool and cotton against her skin. She reached down, with her uninjured arm, and could feel the blankets over her. She reached up and her hand found something like a scarf or towel draped over her face. She felt for its edge and gently pulled it away. She could now see a lantern hanging from a hook in a roof beam. Even though its wick was turned down low, the brightness of even that weak light made her screw up her eyes in discomfort.

Annis felt hot and ill at ease. She took in a lung full of air and found it musty and dank. She exhaled sharply through her nose to expel the odour and immediately heard somebody stir, close by. In a moment, Wild Flower appeared in her field of vision, looking worried.

"Your Majesty?" She whispered.

"Is it day or night?" Annis enquired.

"It is late in the evening, after sundown, Your Majesty."

"Just call me *Ma'am*, if you would," said Annis.

From the briefest flash of emotion on Wild Flower's face, it was clear that she was offended, but she nodded her compliance without complaint.

"Have I been here long?" Annis asked.

"A day and a half, Your…" Wild Flower paused a fleeting second, then hurriedly corrected herself, "Ma'am."

"The horses. The ones who carried me here. Are they well?"

Wild Flower beamed at Annis, her face lighting up with a dazzling smile.

"Yes.... Ma'am! They are well, indeed. Happy to have served you and happy to be rested!"

"Aye," the queen replied, "They must be."

Wild Flower smiled, again, her warmth radiating like a cosy fire.

"They were unhappy," Annis whispered, "On the way here."

"Aye, Ma'am. It grieved them to hurt you with the roughness of the ride."

"You knew that? You could feel it?"

"Aye, Ma'am. They are wise and loving creatures. I can feel their moods and their disposition."

"Yes. A horse is a beautiful thing, for sure."

"I have met many a bad person, Ma'am, but never a bad horse."

Annis could not stop herself from smiling at this response and gave a little chuckle.

"How is my wound?"

Wild Flower screwed up her nose and grimaced.

"I am not as happy with it as I would like to be. I have cleaned it and I have put an ointment on it and some healing herbs and moss..."

"But?"

"But, Ma'am, it is slow to come right."

"It feels hot," Annis complained, "At times it's as if it's on fire."

Wild Flower sighed a long sigh and gave a little irritated gurgle.

"There are those who say that an angry horse looking at a wound can cause it to fester."

"The horses weren't angry!" Annis protested.

"No, they were not. I was just saying. The old folk say this about wounds to explain them failing to heal."

Annis nodded and looked thoughtful.

"Will my wound fail to heal?"

Wild Flower was silent for a moment before she replied.

"There are other people who say that a good and kindly horse can help a wound to heal with just a look."

Annis nodded, again, looking even more thoughtful.

"What kind of place is this?" Annis asked.

"It is a poor and humble taigh-dubh, Ma'am, a little way from Carrbridge. It was gladly yielded to you by a small holder. He was pleased and honoured to be of service to you."

"Did Gavin press them to accept a coin?"

"Aye, Ma'am, I saw it done."

"Good. I am glad."

"You are a queen, My Lady. You can do exactly as you wish."

Annis looked at Wild Flower sharply, but the girl only replied with her lovely smile.

"With a motion of this little finger," the queen scolded, good naturedly, as she held up the said digit, "I can have a man's head cut from his shoulders."

Annis held up another finger and waggled it.

"And with this one," Annis said, "I can have a man sprung from half a life in a prison cell, to feel the breeze in his hair and the sun on his face."

"I do not doubt it, Ma'am. Not for a second."

"And yet, with all ten fingers together and all ten toes besides, I cannot free myself from the prison of being a queen!"

"You are wise beyond your years, Ma'am."

"As are you!" Annis chuckled, "As are you!"

Wild Flower gave her a little bow.

"This is a taigh-dubh? So, tell me of the horses. They are beyond the curtain, over there?" Annis enquired, gesturing with her working arm to the soiled length of rag that hung down in the shadows, "Or are they outside?"

"The ones who brought you here, Ma'am, are mere strides away from us."

"Good. Then show them my arm, if you will, and let them see the wound."

"It will be as you ask, Ma'am," Wild Flower replied, kicking the foot of a boy who slept nearby.

The boy awoke, ill tempered, and sat up to give vent to his annoyance, but – on seeing the queen – he shrank back and touched his brow, submissively.

"To your feet, Bobbins," Wild Flower instructed, "Help the queen to stand."

"At once!" Bobbins replied, leaping up.

He rushed to the side of the queen's pallet, but, once there, was seized by a sudden shyness to touch royal flesh.

"Make quicker about yourself," Wild Flower chided, "Don't let your manners freeze your limbs!"

The boy sheepishly grasped Annis beneath her good shoulder, while Wild Flower supported her around her waist. Together, they shuffled the queen over to the filthy curtain that separated the two halves of the building. It was drawn back to reveal the horses, both stood asleep. As the light hit them, dim though it was, the two beasts promptly awoke. They came forward and stood with their heads over the low wall of straw and mud that held them in.

Wild Flower took the queen's arm and carefully removed the bandages. The boy was charged to bring across the lantern and, as its wick was raised, its light flooded the stable area with a wavering orange glow. With great care the healer held out the queen's arm to the horses for inspection. Each of the beasts, in turn, sniffed it with exquisite delicacy, before snorting as if the smell had stung their nostrils.

"They are not pleased," Wild Flower announced.

"If it were their own limb, they would be even less pleased!" The queen smiled.

The horses sniffed again. As they did so, several loose pieces of straw fell from them and wafted down to settle at the edge of the wound. Nobody noticed this happen and, if they had, they would have thought little of it. They would have seen no reason to clean the injured arm, again. There was no knowledge of germs and infection at the time.

Annis was helped back to bed and her arm was dressed, again. Beneath the cotton bandage, drawing on the warmth of her body, the straw began to rot and decay in the wound. Within a few hours, the strands of straw had become mouldy. Within another few hours, the mould developed a green fur around it and drops of clear liquid started to gather at its edges and seep into the wound. By the following morning, the heat of the injury had gone and the germs that had infected it were dead.

Later, as the nerve endings in the damaged flesh began to regenerate and re-join, Annis began to complain that the wound felt prickly, as if she were being stabbed with pins. Wild Flower was delighted, for she knew this to be a good sign. She washed the flesh, picking out the straw and wiping away the mould, before applying a generous layer of honey over it. She bade the queen be patient and, by the following morning, her arm gave her no pain when she moved it.

CHAPTER 37

The queen's troops had become bored and fractious from being camped too long in the same, inhospitable place. They were gleeful to learn that they could move on.

Balgair and Gavin had been constant visitors to the queen's bedside and their eagerness and persistence was such – according to Wild Flower – that they had quickly become a nuisance. The two men were beyond themselves with joy at the news of Annis' recovery and had hugged and shaken hands – at least twice – with everybody in sight!

A little later, Annis caught Balgair and Gavin dressing up in their best tunics, kilts and sandals in a distinctly celebratory mood.

"Where are the two of you planning to be going, dressed up in all your best, like that?" Annis demanded, pretending to be displeased.

"We are going to gather up some sacks of rocks and stones, then we will climb the tall hill over yonder, and make a cairn at its top so that we can pray and give thanks to God for your return to good health," Balgair announced, piously.

"I thank you," Annis told them, "But I can think of a far better way to give thanks, if you were to think it a fitting thing to do."

"Ask anything!" Gavin replied.

"Anything at all!" Balgair enthused.

Annis now looked at Balgair and, as she took in his handsome face, his powerful arms and his broad chest, she became a little shy and felt a pinkness come to her cheeks.

"I thank you, Sir," she said, quietly.

Suddenly, Balgair could no longer meet her eyes and stood fidgeting, a hint of pink in his own cheeks. Gavin looked away, making a pretence of having to re-strap his sandals.

"I think it would please God more if you were to send some of your quickest and nimblest men, especially those good with a bow or spear, to go and hunt down a couple of boar or deer. Then have them divide up the carcasses between the villages and hamlets around these parts. Tell them to give extra to those who are sick or elderly and to those folks with young children."

Balgair saluted her, without making eye contact, and went about rounding up his troops for the job. Annis watched him walk away, not shifting her gaze until he had gone out of sight. Gavin approached her and bowed.

"He is a fine young man," he said, innocently.

Annis could not stop herself from fully blushing, but then quickly adjusted her face to be formal and composed.

"Yes, I am sure he is," Annis responded, doing her best to sound matter of fact.

Gavin gave a barely visible smile and his eyes twinkled. Annis gave him a stern look and his smile disappeared... at least from his lips.

"Your Majesty," said Gavin, after a pause, "I would be most grateful if you would indulge me by coming and making your presence known to your servants and close aides. They have been most worried for your wellbeing."

"Yes, of course," she replied, inattentively, her thoughts clearly elsewhere.

Annis was standing looking in the direction that Balgair had gone and she seemed to be deep in thought. After waiting for a minute, Gavin cleared his throat and her attention returned.

"Yes!" The queen said, a little too sharply, "I shall see them right away."

Annis began to walk with him and then suddenly stopped.

"What of our forces?" She asked, looking worried, "How did we fare in the battle?"

"In the two battles, we lost six of the twenty troops from your own caravan, My Lady, and twenty-two of the MacDonald and McRory soldiers, including one of Balgair's own cavalrymen. We lost a further nineteen from the MacDonald troops, who later arrived to support us. The Grants lost twenty-seven of their own warriors."

Annis closed her eyes and groaned. She then held her head in her hands.

"So many lives. So many widows. So many orphans," the queen said, sadly, "So much blood spilled after so many years free of war. It breaks my heart to think of it. The sheer waste of it all."

Gavin nodded, dully, and thought of the men who had perished and who would not be returning home. He thought of the children who would never be held by their father, and wives who would never be hugged by their husbands, again.

"We put the badly injured and dying Campbells to the sword, for the most part, along with their collaborators," Gavin announced, "We executed their leaders. We executed those who fought on and would not yield. We executed those we caught who had fled and would not heed our call to stop."

"Did you slay many oath breakers?"

"Aye, Your Majesty, and we then – as required – tossed a coin and slew either the man to their left or the man to their right, according to how it fell."

Annis nodded, sorrowfully, for she derived no pleasure from the taking of life, no matter who the enemy.

"Were there many who broke their oath to us?"

"Aye, My Lady, there was a square dozen. These are, after all, Campbells," replied Gavin, spitting on the ground to show his contempt.

"We have offered the oath, still, to all who would take it?"

"Aye, Your Majesty, we have. Those who laid down their arms were offered the self-same oath of neutrality. If they would forfeit the top of a little finger, above its last joint, and pledge never to raise a sword against you, again, they were spared. Those who declined the bargain were duly slain."

"What of the bodies of the Campbell dead?"

Gavin clenched his teeth and pursed his lips, a silent snarl taking a grip of his mouth.

"The survivors were allowed to bury their dead," Gavin replied, with bitter resentment, "In obedience to **your** wish and **your** command, Your Majesty."

Annis stopped and, turning with deliberate slowness, looked at him with a cool, level gaze. The unspoken rebuke had the desired effect.

"Every one of them, Your Majesty," Gavin assured her, "Now resides beneath the soil."

Annis nodded.

"Our men were not pleased?"

"No, Your Majesty, they were not," Gavin advised, "They were of a mind to string up the Campbell dead from the branches of the trees for the crows to eat, since that would have been their own fate if their roles were reversed."

They resumed walking and said no more to each other until they heard the sound of a river.

"Where is the water I can hear?" Annis asked.

"Beyond the trees, Your Majesty, down the path just ahead of us."

"Wait for me, Gavin, please."

"Your wish is my command."

Annis went down to the water. Gavin sent Bobbins to hide, nearby her, with instructions to call out loudly if an enemy were spotted. Gavin stood watch on the main path and allowed two of the McRory Honour Guard to take up position in the trees to make her more safe, still.

Annis made her way to the water's edge and knelt on the fine sand that bordered it. She reached into the leather bag she kept tied at her waist, beneath her tunic, and took out a scrap of cloth from it. She kissed the shard of material and cast it into the water.

"Dear God," she said, "I cast into the water this fragment of material that I have worn and which may have absorbed my spirit or the essence of my being and I ask that you allow it to convey my prayer to the ocean, into the darkness of its oblivion, and, from there, into the light of your glorious eternity. Please bless my mother, Cydara, taken from us before her time, and let her dwell with You in paradise."

She watched as the piece of drab cotton drifted away downstream and, once it was out of sight, she walked back up the path to where Gavin stood, patiently waiting.

They walked on in silence.

When they reached the tents where her retinue were camped, the cries of joy and exultation were loud and fervent. People ran to her as children might run to their mother. Some wept openly and many raised passionate prayers of thanks and praised various deities for her life.

A fire was lit and big pots of stew were hoisted over them. Two men produced fiddles and began to play in her honour. The jubilation was raucous, wild and enthusiastic. The celebrations went on well beyond midnight and into the small hours of the next morning.

As people started to wander back to their tents, Balgair and Gavin sat together, poking the embers of the once enormous fire with the ends of a pair of sticks.

"You know that the Campbells won't give up, don't you?" asked Gavin.

"Aye, I do," replied Balgair, "They won't stop trying to kill her."

"Today's battle is won, but there will be another – as sure as night follows day – be it in days, be it in weeks or be it in months."